COME TO THE WINDOW

COME

TO THE

WINDOW

A Novel

Howard Norman

W. W. NORTON & COMPANY
Independent Publishers Since 1923

Copyright © 2024 by Howard Norman

All rights reserved
Printed in the United States of America
First Edition

For information about permission to reproduce selections from this book, write to Permissions, W. W. Norton & Company, Inc., 500 Fifth Avenue, New York, NY 10110

For information about special discounts for bulk purchases, please contact W. W. Norton Special Sales at specialsales@wwnorton.com or 800-233-4830

Manufacturing by Lakeside Book Company
Book design by Beth Steidle
Production manager: Devon Zahn

ISBN 978-1-324-07633-9

W. W. Norton & Company, Inc., 500 Fifth Avenue, New York, N.Y. 10110
www.wwnorton.com

W. W. Norton & Company Ltd., 15 Carlisle Street, London W1D 3BS

1 2 3 4 5 6 7 8 9 0

for Andrea Serota and Rick Winston

Come to the window, sweet is the night-air!

—MATTHEW ARNOLD

COME TO THE WINDOW

WHALE INTERVENES ON
WEDDING NIGHT

Journal entry April 28, 1918. 3:30 a.m. Parrsboro

"Whale Intervenes on Wedding Night"
"Murder"
"Universal Stenotype Machine"
"Pocket Diaries"
"Urgent Language"

ON HIS FIRST POSTING AS A COURT STENOGRA-
pher, Peter Lear immediately got it wrong. And I mean in the
first thirty seconds.

Three days ago, I was dispatched by the *Evening Mail* from
Halifax to Parrsboro. In this small fishing outport set along the
Bay of Fundy, I'm covering a preliminary hearing whose sole pur-
pose is to determine if the facts warrant a full trial in the Provin-
cial Court. It's all up to Byron Spencer, the presiding magistrate.
Here is what I know so far.

Elizabeth Frame is accused of murdering her husband, Everett Dewis. The incident took place on the night of April 22,
roughly eleven hours after they had exchanged marriage vows at
St. George's Anglican Church. I was allowed to see their room
on the top floor of Ottawa House, at Partridge Island situated
right at the mouth of Parrsboro Harbor. That fateful night,
the newlyweds' twin dormer windows overlooked a moonlit
bay. It was a room traditionally reserved for visiting dignitar-
ies, which had been few. Lucy Maud Montgomery slept there
when, in the summer of 1908, she'd come to read from *Anne of
Green Gables* at the Anglican Girls' School on Victoria Street.
The room has a four-poster bed. Also a botanical border quilt,
and otherwise white bedclothes. It has a claw-foot bathtub in
a private bathroom. It has an armoire and bedside candles. In
fact, I described the décor when I filed today's coverage with

my editor, Albanie Musgrave, who wired directly back saying she was giving me one column only, with the heading "Whale Intervenes on Wedding Night."

I'm writing this by candlelight in room 103 of Gillespie House Inn, right in the village. The inn is temporarily closed to the public. Upstairs in room 210, Elizabeth Frame herself is under what might be called house arrest; there's three men from Truro hired to sit in six-hour shifts outside her door. These stolid fellows—Mr. Astoria, Mr. Brewster, Mr. Solton—alternately sleep in room 208, which has twin beds. Byron Spencer is on the third floor in room 301, and his assistant Bevel Cousins is in 304. The stenographer Peter Lear is down the corridor from me in 109. That's the nighttime configuration here in Gillespie House Inn.

Today it was "balmy for nearly May," as I overheard, and I'm told that there have been outlandish cloud skirmishes every morning for two weeks now. Yet there's been only slight rain, the Bay of Fundy has been relatively calm, and the nights have been clear.

I cannot wait a moment longer to mention the unusual-most-of-all phenomenon. Which is a whale presently rotting on the beach, all but constantly attended by carrion gulls. In fact, it had washed up on Mr. and Mrs. Dewis's wedding night, not a hundred meters from Ottawa House. I've been to see the whale. It's right there in front of the wooden pilings, either bloated or collapsed depending on which precinct of its bulk and length, whether flukes, gullied throat pleats, dorsal ridge, or pale underside. A clothespin pinched my nostrils closed, but still one has to breathe. Lord have mercy, some dogs have had at the whale. Crows, too. A portion for foxes. But predominantly gulls. And that many gulls can be deafening. It is a gargantuan sad corpse and I found it difficult to imagine it swimming freely, a Vessel of Eternity, as Herman Melville put it, through the watery depths. Standing there, stunned at how puny the human species is, I thought of what my wife Amelia Morley said after she'd read *Moby-Dick*: "It seems that Mr. Melville has written the lost final chapter of the Old Testament."

I miss my wife terribly. Schooled in London, she was the first-ever woman to be resident surgeon at Victoria General Hospital. But for the past six months now she's been in Arques and Étaples in France, working with the No. 7 Stationary Hospital, out of Dalhousie University. In a letter she wrote, "Toby, my love, I've seen things I never could imagine, let alone that I'd actually see. Influenza is everywhere like an invisible demon. And here in Étaples, young men and older men are patients, ruins of their former physical selves, so many amputations, broken, fever-ridden. Mustard gas coughs heard all night. We even have German sick and wounded. Men ask me to pray with them, though I feel as if I merely get through prayer rather than believe in it, even on their behalf. But every so often I'm convinced. I've even been asked to write to their families."

The whale's eyes were filmed over. A local fisherman, Petrus Dollard, told me, "This past Sunday the whale's stench broadcast up to St. John's Anglican Church, so that some parishioners departed mid-sermon. Rector Thomas Shrevard was none too happy about that."

For a decade now, I've covered such hearings in every corner of the province. I keep one notebook for the odd thought, another notebook for interviews, and a third for little maps of whatever village. In the time allowed, you must try to notice, eavesdrop on, and learn everything possible; Albanie likes to use the word "sleuthing."

From what I've learned, just from day one of the hearing, the whale might be seen as the start of Elizabeth Frame's mortal difficulties. What's more, I contend that the very sight of this whale summoned up dramatic aspects of Elizabeth's soul, mind, and spirit. Why do I suggest such a thing? Because in the witness chair Elizabeth herself talked about her murderous act as if it were a biblical moment. For example, she said that she'd risen from the bed "naked as Eve," looked out the window, and thereby saw the "spectacle of a leviathan, as if torn from the Book of Psalms." She then had studied the whale for a few moments, even said a prayer for it. And it was at this point, by her estimation somewhere around 4 a.m., she had said, "Darling, come to the window. A whale has intervened on our wedding night." But Everett Dewis refused her request, and a certain "rage of disappointment" overtook her. So that when Everett fluffed the pillow in a deliberate way that had reminded Elizabeth of someone playing a few quick notes on the accordion (she demonstrated this), yawned, and then turned away from her, Elizabeth promptly went into his leather satchel, removed his military revolver, and said, "Everett, here comes a dry morsel . . ." and shot him "three times in the body." She then threw on Everett's nightshirt and went down to visit the whale.

By the way, that thing Elizabeth said, "Everett, here comes a dry morsel . . ." My room has a King James Bible and I finally found the passage I was looking for, in Proverbs 17:1. *Better is a dry morsel, and quietness therewith, than a house full of sacrifices with strife.*

A dry morsel; a bullet.

⁓

HOWEVER, AS COMPELLING AS "Darling, come to the window" was, they weren't the first words Elizabeth uttered in the witness chair, in the spacious dining room of Ottawa House Inn that had become a makeshift courtroom. And therefore they weren't the first words Peter Lear recorded. No, the instant she sat down (according to my pocket watch, 9:15 a.m.) in the ladder-back chair provided by Josephine Huntley, the proprietor of Ottawa House, Elizabeth Frame, unprompted, said, "The saddest part was, just a few hours before I killed my new husband, in our matrimonial bed there'd been contrapuntal moans." (I doubt that Everett Dewis would have found *that* the saddest part.) Obviously, in saying what she'd said, Elizabeth had outright confessed to the murder, and now all that was left to hear was how—and maybe a little of why—it had come about. It was as if everyone in the makeshift courtroom had to abruptly detour their curiosities from one mystery to another. I actually jotted down *contrapuntal* in my notebook and followed it with a big question mark. In my line of work I'm hardly a stranger to the English language, but I had no earthly idea what *contrapuntal* meant.

Apparently neither did Magistrate Spencer. He was dressed in a well-traveled black suit, white shirt buttoned at the neck. A lanky fellow about age fifty-five, I would guess, with a kind of asymmetrical face, decidedly more vertical in structure than rounded, a luxurious head of thick black hair flecked white at the sideburns, very kind brown eyes, spectacles. Anyway, Spencer stopped the proceedings. He turned to his assistant and said, "Mr. Cousins, find me a dictionary." In about fifteen minutes,

Bevel Cousins had found a dictionary in the Anglican Girls' School and delivered it to the magistrate. Spencer had remained seated behind his desk with his eyes closed. I thought he might be taking a brief nap, but more plausibly that was how he retreated inward. "Thank you, Mr. Cousins," he said. He then paged through the dictionary.

(By the way, I'm pretty sure that Byron Spencer, Bevel Cousins, Peter Lear—and myself, Tobias Havenshaw—are the only come-from-aways.) I found it interesting how some eighty or more of Parrsboro's citizens—the population here stands at 357—all the chairs taken and everyone else either sitting atop tables or standing along the walls, seemed united in rapt anticipation of a dictionary definition. I took this as a kind of sympathetic obligation to the accused and her family. You see, Elizabeth had been born and raised in Parrsboro, so everyone knew her. Since age nine she'd been half orphaned; ever since her father, Zachary Frame, was lost at sea, his empty grave has been in New Canaan Cemetery. Whereas her mother, Elsbeth Frame, sat front row not ten meters from the witness chair.

Finally, Magistrate Spencer said, "Don't take this down, Mr. Lear. I'll tell you when to resume recording. I understand you're the first male legal stenographer in the province."

"I believe that's true, Your Honor," Lear said.

"Well, well," Spencer said. "How fortunate for us to have you, Mr. Lear."

"Thank you," Lear said.

"And is that the latest model of Universal Stenotype Machine?" Spencer said.

"Yes, Your Honor, it is," Lear said.

"And was it provided by the province," Spencer said, "and does it come out of your salary?"

"Yes to both," Lear said.

"Well, it's a handsome machine," Spencer said. "It can spell any word in the dictionary to boot."

Apparently Magistrate Spencer had wanted to demonstrate his sense of irony. "You may resume recording," Spencer said. On his desk, Spencer placed his coffee mug so that it propped open the dictionary and read out loud the definition of *contrapuntal*: " 'harmonically interdependent in rhythm and melodic contour.' "

At which point some fellow in the audience called out, "Elizabeth, that word's going to keep me up to all hours of the night!"

Allow me here to be influenced by the fact that Ottawa House Inn is situated so near the Bay of Fundy: a veritable wave of laughter now rolled forth from the audience. Magistrate Spencer let the wave land, as it were, at his feet, before striking the gavel and demanding silence.

He turned to Elizabeth. "Do you have anything to say, Mrs. Dewis?"

"Kindly refer to me as 'Miss Frame,' " Elizabeth said. "And yes, I do have something to say."

"Miss Frame, I only ask that you be civil," Spencer said.

Elizabeth Frame is twenty-four. She has auburn hair cut in a style, as I overheard Josephine Huntley say, not without admiration, "out of a magazine." She has almost an unfair natural beauty, which she seems neither to play up nor to play down. She's slim as a Christmas candle, and is five feet nine inches tall, which I learned from her family physician, Dr. S. S. Particulate, which strikes me as a name the Canadian National Steamship

Company might give to a steamer that makes Atlantic crossings. I would call Elizabeth's pattern of speech noticeable. Many of her sentences resolve in a downward lilt, the weight of the world on her tongue, and therefore whatever she says seems to contain resignation; she may well be a person who, every day, must work herself *up* to melancholy. "Ever since she was a child," Josephine Huntley told me, "Lizzie liked to use big words for things a small word would do." Benefit of the doubt might allow that this was less show-offy than a young girl already attempting to refine her intellect, and courageous enough to do so even in her elementary school classroom. Still, it's true, going by this morning's testimony, her adult speech can seem like a pastiche of antiquities. But maybe she always wanted language to single her out. I consider myself a student of people; I like to think about such things. With Elizabeth Frame, of course, this is all just first impressions on my part.

All the same, I've found that some people exhibit their temperaments in an immediately memorable fashion. I feel that Elizabeth is one of those. For instance, I learned from Bevel Cousins that in a preliminary interview, when Magistrate Spencer asked if her childhood was happy or unhappy, Elizabeth had replied, "By this moody, tremulous ocean I've always lived intensely." And Elizabeth's own mother said, "Lizzie often got words and phrases from poetry, hymns, and eventually novels, but she used them in a surprising way." I also learned from Elsbeth that at age eleven Elizabeth had said to Rector Shrevard, "When I get older I'm going to write stories, and you should know I listen closely to every word of your fine sermons. So I'm putting what you say in the bank, and I'll be able to withdraw it whenever I want." Her mother then added that throughout her childhood, Elizabeth was expert at neatly tucking a warning into a compliment, which I thought was nicely put.

In the witness chair Elizabeth chose to wear the dress she was married to Everett Dewis in, a Victorian-style cream-colored muslin two-piece with ten buttons up front, wide embroidered lapels, a silk bow in back, and a floral pattern on the sleeves and at the collar. Wearing her wedding dress for a hearing about murdering her husband on their wedding night was one of the most off-slant exhibits of pathos I'd ever experienced in a courtroom. She had to have put a lot of thought into wearing that dress.

Looking down at her hands clasped together as if she was praying, Elizabeth thought for a moment and finally said, "You see, Everett and I moaned in ways that I described as *contrapuntal*, because I'd been taking mail-order music composition lessons and recently had a whole new vocabulary."

Magistrate Spencer hit the desk with his gavel, which stopped more laughter before it had even begun. He grimaced warningly at the audience.

"Does your music composition teacher have a name?" he said.

"Yes, his name is Oscar Asch," she said. "He lives in Halifax. He's Bavarian by birth. But he's applied to become a Canadian citizen."

"On principle always a good idea," Spencer said.

Elizabeth hesitated a moment, then delivered a real wallop of a fact: "It was Oscar Asch who picked out and provided my wedding dress, which I'm presently wearing," she said. "All at his own expense. The dress was part of his own proposal of marriage to me. He's a widower, you see. What's more, Oscar had no knowledge of my previous engagement to Everett Dewis. I'm sure none of this reflects well on me. But the dress fits nicely, don't you think?"

It took a moment, through the collective inward gasps and murmurs and one "Oh my!" before Magistrate Spencer struck his gavel again. The room hushed right down.

I wrote in my notebook: *She married Everett Dewis—she was in love with someone else? What is going on here?*

Elizabeth forged ahead. "Around five weeks or so before I married Everett, I made a visit to Halifax. I'd told my mother that it was to pick out my wedding dress. She wanted to accompany me in this endeavor, as any mother would, but I insisted that I wanted the adventure of the city on my own. I hadn't been there before, you see. And in Halifax I rendezvoused with Oscar Asch. A rendezvous that lasted three whole nights, with the days spent together in between."

"And how long had these mail-order lessons been taking place?" Spencer said.

"Five months. In total Oscar Asch and I have exchanged eight letters," Elizabeth said. "That is perfectly equal at four each. You can pack a lot of hopes and dreams in a letter, did you know that?"

"I'll want to examine Mr. Asch's letters," Magistrate Spencer said.

"I hereby give my mother permission to provide them," Elizabeth said. "By the way, my mother approved of the dress. Of course, she thought I'd picked it out myself."

Peter Lear is age twenty-seven and was born in Sydney Mines, Nova Scotia. I know for a fact that in 1916 he was inducted into the 25th Battalion, Nova Scotia Regiment, Canadian Expeditionary Force. He fought in France and was wounded in November 1917, at the Battle of Passchendaele in Belgium—he uses a cane to compensate his right side. He shipped home in January 1918 and passed his court stenographic exam in March.

I noticed that Lear crouched forward at the Universal Stenotype, his face set with an almost comical determination. To me it looked a little painful. Benefit of the doubt dictates—no pun intended—that I take into consideration how new he is to the profession; even his posture is apprenticing. All right, a young man wanting to be good at his job, to lean into it, should not be faulted for that. In his dark brown corduroy suit and trousers, too heavy for spring, Lear was formal if threadbare; he also wore a white shirt and taupe necktie loose at the knot. He had noticeably scuffed shoes.

Lear is just short, by American measure, of six feet in height, I'd guess. I could well imagine that even if receiving the much-needed attentions of a barber, his dark brown hair might retain a restless aspect. He has brown eyes, he might consciously dress to match his eyes, I couldn't possibly know. He has a downward smile. Overall, Lear is what Amelia might describe as "handsome in a careless way," that is, unaffected. A rather interesting man to look at and take in, I feel.

Some men and women continue to evidence their youthful physiognomy well into middle age (for example, when my wife Amelia smiles, she seems to be smiling out of a photograph of herself at age twelve) or even old age, but I would have to predict the opposite will be true of Peter Lear. His exhausted expressions seem to forecast how his looks will eventually settle. I suppose that this is merely advance notice of the fate of the body. Amelia might say that Lear "looks beyond his years."

"Mr. Lear, please scroll back the tape and read the testimony from the beginning," Magistrate Spencer said.

I must confess that at this point Peter Lear drew my utmost sympathy, and in fact I cringed on his behalf when shortly after he'd followed Magistrate Spencer's instruction. Lear cleared his throat and read, "'The saddest part was, just before I killed my new husband, in our matrimonial bed there'd been contrapuntal moons...'"

Whether Lear had mistakenly written *contrapuntal moons*, and therefore had read it correctly, or whether he'd simply mispronounced *moans*, I did not know. Either way, no amount of gavel pounding could fend off the ensuing laughter. It just went on and on. Even Elizabeth Frame shook her head back and forth, incredulous. Peter Lear had, in equal measure, a look of despair and embarrassment. He tried to carry on with reading the transcript, but Spencer said, "Mr. Lear, it's fine, please cease and desist, it's all right. it's fine."

The gavel took effect this time. "Mr. Lear," Spencer said, "you do realize, don't you, that at night when we gaze at the heavens, we are able to see only the *one* moon."

"I do realize that," Lear said.

"I'm so relieved," Spencer said. He flicked through the dictionary, stopped at a page, and read, "'*Erratum:* an error in speech or printing.' Let's call it an erratum, then."

Speechless, Peter Lear stared into the middle distance. But the proceedings had gone off the rails, and Spencer did the correct thing by saying, "Let's resume this hearing tomorrow morning at nine a.m."

Spencer left the dining room. He'd put in about two hours of work for the taxpayers of the province. As for Peter Lear, when he stood up from his chair, he knocked the stenograph machine off its stand, though managed to catch it, and thus spared himself more humiliation. It's a particularly fragile instrument, I'm told. Bevel Cousins escorted Elizabeth Frame from the room— she embraced her mother on the way—and then the rest of us filed out of Ottawa House.

⁓

COFFEE AND A CHEESE SANDWICH for lunch in my room. Then I spent some of the afternoon talking to people. I had particularly hoped to track down anyone who might have seen Elizabeth immediately after the gunshots. Often the kind of long articles I write for the crime pages of the *Evening Mail* become part of the forensics of communal memory. But today I only found one eyewitness, Josephine Huntley. I'd heard she often burned the midnight oil, doing paperwork and whatnot in her office. I found her there on the first floor of Ottawa House.

Josephine is approaching stout and is ambidextrous, which I imagine sounds no more than disparate elements, but were things I noticed and learned right off. When I walked into her office, she was pecking away one-fingered on a typewriter with her right hand while drinking a cup of tea with her left.

"Want to see me type with my left hand?" she said.

"No thank you," I said.

"Because I'm known for typing with either hand," she said.

She looked relaxed in a kind of housedress, and her dark brown hair fairly cascaded to shoulder-length, framing her pleasant face. Her voice was gravelly, but I didn't know whether that was its natural timbre or if she was suffering a sore throat or worse. When she coughed a little, she said, "Don't be alarmed, it's not Spanish flu. In fact, there's nothing Spanish in Parrsboro. I've been to the doctor. It's not influenza. These days, you get even the slightest headache, you worry until the doctor says elsewise."

I introduced myself and said, "I heard you're a night owl, and so I had thought you just possibly might've seen Elizabeth Frame after the gunshots."

Stiffly cordial at first, she said she'd "not resist" talking about what she'd seen the night of the murder. "Not resist" had a touch of ambivalence about it, but I was a total stranger to her, what should've I expected?

"I'll provide some facts but no personal emotions," she said.

"How's that?"

"That would be fine."

"I'm a friend of the family, after all," she said. "Zachary Frame, for instance—Lizzie's father—is sacred to the memory, poor man."

"I understand."

"Well, whether you do or not, go on, ask your question."

Right away I noticed a telescope in the corner of her cluttered room. "Do you like stargazing?"

"It's quite simple. Amateur astronomy is welcome on a sleepless night."

"Mrs. Huntley, were you by any chance stargazing on the night of the murder?"

"Of course, I heard the gunshots. But before that, I'd been so busy looking at the Ursus Major constellation, I didn't even notice God's largest creature tumble onto the beach. Distracted by the heavens, you might say. It was only seeing Lizzie Frame walk right past my window on the porch here, wearing a nightshirt and looking preternatural. That's when I properly adjusted my telescope and followed her down the beach. She was holding the revolver, in her right hand. Though she's left-handed."

"What happened next?"

"What happened next I will never forget. I just will never forget it."

"I'm all ears."

"Lizzie stood with her forehead pressed against the whale. Through the telescope I saw her mouth moving, like she was talking to the creature. And then she climbed up along the tail, keeping her balance, keeping her balance, keeping her balance. She mainly on all fours got to the blowhole. And then she pressed the revolver right down into it. It was a once-in-a-lifetime sight, that's for sure. That exact thing just cannot have happened before and won't again, because Mr. Havenshaw, how could it? But God as my witness, that is what happened."

Distraught to the point of tears, Josephine Huntley, without another word, stood up and showed me the door.

⁓

I HAD DINNER AT 6 P.M. in the dining room of Ottawa House. There was one cook and one server, a young woman named Rebecca Stock, who was about seventeen or so. Elizabeth Frame sat at a corner table with upright square-shouldered Mr. Astoria and upright square-shouldered Mr. Solton. Still in her wedding dress, Elizabeth looked exhausted and crestfallen as a person could. It would suggest deep suffering, but I didn't know the secret contradictions of her heart, did I. I only knew what I'd heard at the hearing. I only knew she'd murdered her husband.

I only knew she'd just reached over and taken up the remainder of Mr. Solton's steak and potatoes with her fork, eaten it quickly, and still looked famished.

It was at about seven thirty, while sipping whiskey from a glass filched from the dining room, I'd sat propped against pillows in my room, writing in this journal. But after half an hour, tempted to carry out the Devil's errand, as Amelia might say, I carried the bottle down the corridor to Peter Lear's room. There I ran into Rebecca Stock, who was carrying her own bottle of whiskey.

"I'm supposed to deliver this to Mr. Lear," she said. "At his request."

I held up my bottle and said, "All taken care of."

She shrugged and turned back down the corridor.

When I knocked, Lear called through the door, "Thanks, but I've changed my mind."

"Probably a good idea," I said.

Then nothing; then I knocked again.

A moment passed and he opened the door. Peter Lear stood there in his full-length flannel pajamas, worse-for-wear bathrobe, and bedroom slippers. Made himself right at home, I thought. The pajamas not quite right for a fairly warm night. He had a fire going in the small fireplace; considering the corduroy suit he'd worn at the hearing, I wondered if he'd gotten so cold so easily before he suffered the elements in the trenches.

"I recognize you from the hearing," he said. "I'd ordered a bottle of spirits. But I need to be alert tomorrow, so decided against it."

I held up my bottle. "My name's Toby Havenshaw," I said. "From the *Evening Mail*."

"Did you already file for today?"

"Yes."

"And did you include my erratum?"

"No." Now came my first ingratiation. "Just a human mistake."

"What do you want?"

"To ask you some questions, to learn a little about you, Mr. Lear. A little of your story."

"But I'm just the court stenographer. I really don't have anything to do with anything."

Now my second ingratiation. "Only that posterity relies on your gift for urgent language."

He looked puzzled. "All right, come in then."

He turned and went ahead of me. In a glance I noticed a stack of books on top of the bedside table. I noticed pocket diaries. I noticed that everything seemed precisely assigned a place. I thought this may have come from military training. Trousers folded. Three shirts on hangers in the closet; when he saw me look, he shut the closet door. What he then said sounded like a quote from literature: "'He dusted the picture frames and watered the plants on the sill, though out the window, he could see the enemy fleet fast approaching.'"

The bed was all hospital corners. A book lay open facedown on the table next to an easy chair. A candle was lit to read by. And there was a vial of pills, I imagined for his leg, but possibly for nerves. I picked up the book and saw it was a collection of the fragments of Heraclitus.

"That book got me through nearly ten months of hell in France and Belgium," he said. "Turn to page 107." I did that and saw in the lower left corner a slightly smudged fingerprint, whose whorls appeared to be blood-dried. "That's from the thumb of my dearest friend, Private Sebastian Lamartine. We grew up together in Sydney Mines. After we took a particularly merciless shelling, that's all I have left of him."

The fragment on page 107 read:

The soul is undiscovered
though explored forever
to a depth beyond report

"Well, you might say I'm involved in the report of murder, for some ten years now at the *Evening Mail*," I said. "But I admit I haven't thought much about the soul."

"Why not go back to your room right now and start?"

"If that's what you want. Whose soul should I think about?"

"I don't much care." With his grimace and deep sigh, I knew he regretted having invited me in.

Peter sat down in the easy chair. I sat down in the desk chair. I took a swig from my bottle and then he took a swig. I thought it showed a little promise, considering how finicky he seemed, that he was willing to share a bottle like that.

"In general, though, why Heraclitus?" I said.

"I like Heraclitus because he doesn't tell me how to think. He just gets me to think. Just a day before I was wounded—I've still got shrapnel in my knee—I'd read, *How, from a fire that never sinks or sets, would you escape?* And I suppose having startled awake in mud, then borne off on a stretcher, put into a horse cart, then transported to hospital on roads for three days while in agonizing pain—that was my answer to the question posed by Heraclitus. That's how I escaped."

"You had it tough in Belgium. You survived to tell the tale."

"Tell it to whom? What are you talking about? I don't talk

about it. But seeing I've allowed a newspaper writer into my room, let me turn the tables and ask you a question. When you first saw me sit down at my machine, and throughout the hearing, cut short as it was, what were your impressions?"

"Of you?"

"Yes, seeing it was my first day of that sort of employment."

"I didn't think you were as ... *educated* ... as I now know you are."

"Fact is, I'm educated only through one semester at nonsectarian Dalhousie, grades below average. But I did take a philosophy course from Professor Jonathan Weathers Flynn. I could've used another semester with him, but on came the war."

"I take it Professor Flynn introduced you to Heraclitus."

"Wrong. It was Sebastian Lamartine, my best mate."

" 'Death all around, and yet this one shreds the heart most.' That's from Ivor Gurney."

Peter Lear's expression soured. "Read the soldier-poets while cozily sipping tea at home, did you?" he said. He drank but didn't pass the bottle back, and then half muttered, "You didn't serve, did you."

"The result of childhood rheumatism. Impaired joints. I told them I'd grown out of it. It hardly affects me. I failed the physical. I was refused. I did other things for the war effort."

"I really can't like you, Mr. Havenshaw. Still, I admit something you said got to me—it was that phrase 'urgent language.' How did you mean that?"

"I meant that every word a court stenographer takes down has potential to help determine guilt or innocence. So that is what I call 'urgent language.' It can be life-and-death stuff."

Peter Lear suddenly looked as if he'd gone so far inward that

I might have to call the fire brigade to pulley him out. When I said, "Are you all right?"—he cut me off, with a sideways chop of the air.

"It's not the drink that's got me so sullen," Lear said. "It's what's in these pocket diaries over there." He pointed to a stack of them atop a satchel on the bureau. "Their content is all talking ghosts. I brought them back from France and Belgium. I'm never without them. And I've just now realized that those pocket diaries contain my apprenticeship in urgent language."

"How so?"

"You see, Mr. Havenshaw, I saw action at Passchendaele."

He pulled up his pajama leg to reveal a mangled knee and a main scar and three tributary scars.

"It's nothing that could be imagined by someone who wasn't in it," I said. It was my worst ingratiation. Though I believed what I'd said.

"When my lieutenant found out about the diaries, it fell on me to take down the last words of some in my regiment. Whoever could still talk, that is. 'Please tell my wife . . . please tell my daughter . . . please tell my mother and father . . . please tell my wife.' Fourteen diaries filled with such requests. If you put your ear to someone's mouth like that, you are making a sacred promise to them, Mr. Havenshaw. I consider this my God-given assignment, to try and deliver to as many people as possible what these men said before they died. I intend to start soon as this hearing's over. I've got names and addresses all written out."

"Did you take down last words from just Nova Scotians?"

"One of the stupidest and cruelest questions anyone could ask. Of course not. I just can't see myself traveling outside the province. I won't have the resources."

"Apologies."

"If you use any of this for the *Evening Mail*, I'll want to strangle you." He was slurring his words a little. "I half strangled a Hun soldier. Jammed my rifle butt into his throat. Finally I drowned him in mud."

I held my open-palmed hand up as if swearing on the Bible. "You have my word."

Right then, across from me in the easy chair, Peter Lear dozed off. He sat straight up awake almost right away, though, squinted me back into focus, and said, "Elizabeth is quite pretty, don't you think?" To say the least, this took me aback. The bottle fell to the floor, spilling out onto the braided rug. He was asleep again. I blew out the candle and shut the door behind me.

I might better have returned to my own room, but instead revisited the whale. I'm afraid that I cannot say what drew me there. Maybe I wanted to see it at night because Elizabeth had. I was alone on the beach. From a distance of about twenty meters, a starry night, I could see that on the whale's body archipelagoes of dried sea salt actually sparkled. Loudly accounted for were many gulls. Their voices tore the dark air and all but two or three flew off at my approach. Nothing could dissuade the others. The stench as much cloaked me like some invisible fabric as rioted in my nostrils. Given the world—the slaughter of thousands of men occurring in Europe, the merciless plague of influenza already setting up shop here and there in Canada, even the local murder I'd traveled here to report on—it would, I thought, be easy to experience a general collapse of the spirit.

I looked across to the third floor of Ottawa House. The darkened glass of the dormer windows.

Shades of light and darkness moved across the water. I believe that I stayed nearly an hour with the whale. So many lights on in houses, lanterns, candles. You notice such a thing far less in the city. I remember my father saying, "People have trouble sleeping for every imaginable and unimaginable reason. Don't judge."

Back in Gillespie House Inn, I stripped off my clothes. Scrubbed and bathed in the bathtub, I'm back now at this desk with my journal. I think I see a scribbled line of magenta and pink sunrise, far out on the horizon. But it may be a trick of light. What stupid hope guarantees us another day of life? I miss Amelia very much. Before dousing the candle, I need to jot down a separate note: *WHY IS THE NAME OSCAR ASCH SO FAMILIAR TO ME?*

SMITHEREENS

Journal entry April 30, 1918. 2:25 a.m. Parrsboro

"Second Day of Hearing"
"Whale Is Blown to Smithereens by Naval Demolitionist"
"Fatalities in Parrsboro"
"Amelia Is Home from the War"

OSCAR ASCH, OSCAR ASCH. I COULD NOT GET THE name out of my head. Yesterday morning first thing I asked Mrs. Huntley to send a wire from her desk at Ottawa House to my editor Albanie Musgrave, asking her to check if there is a file on Oscar Asch. I had a scone and coffee at Harbor Bakery. Mrs. Huntley found me there and handed me Albanie's response.

"I read both yours and the one you got back," she said. "You're not the only busybody in Parrsboro. Except you're getting paid for it."

"True enough," I said.

"Three things you should know. The hearing today doesn't begin till one o'clock. Secondly, there's a photographer from Truro taking pictures of the whale this morning, maybe as we speak. Name's Victor Alt."

"I'd like to see that."

"Thirdly, the village saw fit to hire a naval demolitionist to dispatch the whale. He's due here around noon. His name is Elliot Hubbard. Much decorated in the war."

"Photographer. Demolitionist. Thanks, Mrs. Huntley."

"You can't claim nothing goes on in Parrsboro, can you? Today, for instance, is going to be busy as any day in the Old Testament."

"I've never thought about how busy a day in the Old Testament was."

"Well, I think about it all the time."

Mrs. Huntley left the bakery and I read the wire:

```
I DON'T HAVE INFLUENZA STOP NOT THAT YOU ASKED
STOP AS FOR OSCAR ASCH STOP YOUR OWN ARTICLE ON
THE SEDITION ACT MENTIONS HIM STOP OSCAR ASCH
BORN IN BAVARIA 1875 STOP MIGRATED TO NOVA SCOTIA
1900 STOP EMPLOYMENT PRIVATE PIANO LESSIONS STOP
STARTED MAIL-ORDER MUSIC COMPOSITION LESSONS STOP
BUSINESS PARTNER WIFE LEONI STOP WIFE DIED IN
1908 STOP "BLOOD DISEASE" STOP 1916 ASCH DETAINED
UNDER WAR MEASURES ACT FOR SEDITION UTTERING PRO-
GERMAN SYMPATHIES IN PUBLIC STOP DENIED LEGAL
REPRESENTATION STOP RELEASED FROM PRISON IN JUST
NINE DAYS STOP HOW'S MURDER IN THE OUTPORTS? STOP
NEXT TIME ASK AFTER MY HEALTH STOP MUSGRAVE
```

Ah, so that's where I heard the name.

It was a brisk clear morning. The Bay of Fundy was bright blue and there were whitecaps. At the wharf was a gathering of about fifty people. A few horse-and-buggy were drawn up on the beach. I stood atop the pilings; a fellow there said, "Air's boldly perfumed, eh?" I would guess there were at least fifteen variously aged boys who stood cavorting fore and aft on the whale carcass, which I found undignified toward Nature. Someone had set a crank-handle phonograph on the sand. It was playing hymns. To me this was a desperate attempt to add spiritual gravitas to the strangely festive scene, but the soaring voices were scratchy, and at one point a gull landed directly on the phonograph, spread its wings, and pecked violently at the phonograph record, making it skip hymn to hymn.

There was only one fishing boat at anchor, *D. R. Kimber's Weeping Mermaid*; on deck was the photographer Victor Alt.

From my vantage point, I saw that Alt was about forty years old, with thick black hair under a black wide-brimmed fedora, and he wore a black greatcoat, which looked ungainly, but he moved easily inside it. He had a handheld camera with a guillotine shutter. He had a brown suitcase that lay open at his feet. It was full of items I couldn't see in detail. Tilting his body left and right, crouching, he took his photographs.

When he finished his work, Alt climbed down into a dinghy and rowed to shore. Once on solid land, Alt vomited; someone near me said, "Seasick on a boat sitting in harbor, now that's one for the books." A buggy pulled right up, and I later found out it was driven by his daughter Abigail. Alt set his suitcase and camera and everything else in back, stood on the bed of the truck, and spoke through a megaphone: "This is *Victor Alt Everyday Photographs and Family Portraits*. Located in Truro. I am locally represented now by Mrs. Huntley, whom you all know. Photographs of your whale will be one dollar each. But of course I am giving one to the town, gratis. I have left my card at Ottawa House. Thank you for the fine opportunity here." Alt then sat down holding the megaphone as Abigail navigated the buggy up to the road, and then they were gone. I made a note to order a photograph and to put it on my expense account from the *Evening Mail*.

I then tried to get some interviews. When I walked just west of the village and knocked on the door of Mr. Fred Dewis and his wife Marigold Oliver Dewis—Everett's parents—nobody answered. I saw Marigold part the curtains and take my measure. Then she opened the door and said, "We pray for Everett but not for Elizabeth. Guess for the time being that makes us only half Christian."

Because she had made the effort to open the door to say what she said, I understood that she needed to slam the door in my face, which she did.

Fred suddenly appeared at the side of the house. "You only experienced Marigold's directness," he said. "But if you come back, you'll experience something more memorable."

Next, across the village, I managed to get a fifteen-minute audience with Elsbeth Frame. She served me tea in her drawing room. She sat stiffly upright. No tea for herself.

"I already said quite enough about my daughter Lizzie in my prayers today," she said.

"Life must be very painful for you just now."

She cringed and shook her head slowly back and forth. I'm sure that pretty much anything I said would have seemed obsequious.

"I'm uncomfortable with you," she said. "But I'll offer you one regret other than inviting you in for tea. Then you'll have to leave. I should have insisted on chaperoning Lizzie in Halifax. Yes, I should have. And I'll never forgive myself for not. But her young heart shouted down all reason. She felt something awaited her there and her mind was made up. And once my daughter's mind is made up, why, the Devil himself better just curtsy and step aside."

Elsbeth Frame stood and went into her bedroom and closed the door. I took up my notebook, set the teacup and saucer next to the kitchen sink, and left the house. These were what I would call unsuccessful interviews. No lunch for me; I walked to the hearing.

∽

BY ROUGH COUNT, there were at least two dozen more people crowded into the dining room of Ottawa House than on the first day of the hearing. There was a low murmuring hum of talk and laughter, everyone waiting for Spencer's gavel. I stood along the wall left of the magistrate's table. Scanning the room, I noticed that Fred and Marigold Dewis were absent. Elsbeth Frame was again sitting directly in front of the witness chair. Her face was full of anguish, I'd say. Her white and gray hair was braided in a tight bun atop her head. She had a lap full of knitting and kept her head down as she started in on the sleeve of a sweater.

Of whom I came to think of as the principal figures, Peter Lear was the first to appear. He wore the exact same clothes as he had yesterday. He looked unkempt and sleep deprived, and of course I knew the reason. We caught each other's eye and he nodded to me, but I couldn't read his expression. Maybe there was nothing to read. He was unshaven and his hair badly combed. When Magistrate Spencer walked in through the kitchen door and sat behind his desk, he studied Lear for a moment and finally said, "Well, Mr. Lear, up to all hours memorizing the dictionary, were we?" But Peter just kept cleaning the stenographic machine with an oiled piece of cloth, and neither looked up nor replied.

Bevel Cousins escorted Elizabeth in, and by "escorted," I mean he was deferential; he held her right elbow lightly, but at the same time had his left hand firmly planted on her left shoulder. She did look a touch wobbly. Today Elizabeth wore a black-and-white-striped bustle dress. When she stepped up to the witness chair, she turned, balletically on tiptoes, in a slow circle, and said, "Also sent by Oscar Asch!" The woman standing next to me said, "Gussied up for the occasion. But I sort of miss the wedding dress." I noticed that Elizabeth was in stockinged feet.

Magistrate Spencer looked no-nonsense. He hit the gavel

only once on his desk. According to my pocket watch it was 1:25. Peter looked at the ready.

"I've been curious, Miss Frame," Spencer said. "Where's the murder weapon?"

Elizabeth rose to this question, straightening her back, looking directly at Spencer. "I stuffed it down the blowhole of the whale," she said, matter-of-factly.

"I beg your pardon?"

"I stuffed it down the blowhole of the whale."

"Oh, come now, Miss Frame."

From the far left of the first row of chairs, Josephine Huntley spoke up. "She's telling the truth! I saw it all through my telescope."

"Good Lord—" Spencer said. "A piece of evidence to be retrieved how, I wonder."

"Yes, where's Jonah when we need him!" some fellow called out from the audience, which drew a lot of laughter. Spencer used his gavel to full effect. Things calmed down.

"All right," Spencer said, "let's move on. Miss Frame, I've spent time with the letters you received from Mr. Oscar Asch."

"Letters to win a woman's heart," Elizabeth said.

"Your mother assures me she hasn't read them," he said. Spencer slid out a letter from an envelope. "This is from a letter dated April 14 of this year." He read with no flair: "'My darling, I enclose your copy of our marriage certificate.'" Spencer then held up the marriage certificate itself, putting it on display, as if to share his incredulousness. And then Spencer said, "I've examined this document. It's authentic."

You could have heard a pin drop.

"But do you have an actual question for me?" Elizabeth said.

"I think it's more the order of events," Spencer said. "As evidenced by this marriage certificate, you and Mr. Oscar Asch were married on March 11 of this year. Officiated by justice of the peace Vincent Carrier. Then, on April 22nd of this year, you married Everett Dewis, in the St. John Anglican Church, here in Parrsboro. How on earth am I supposed to understand this?"

"I'm nothing if not impetuous," Elizabeth said.

"Unwelcome sarcasm. Unwelcome."

"I am also with child."

There was a loud explosion. It rattled the windows of Ottawa House. "That's got to be the whale!" some fellow shouted.

I had been looking at Peter Lear; when the explosion shook the building, he threw himself to the floor. It was reflexive—if that's the right word—it had to be from the trenches. It had to be from Passchendaele.

"Let's try and stay calm," Spencer said loudly, banging his gavel. "Let's stay nice and calm."

But when Petrus Dollard burst into the dining room, stood on a table, and announced, "There's been a terrible accident. The demolitionist Mr. Hubbard has blown himself and the whale to smithereens," straightaway people began to leave the room, abandoning one tragedy for another, you might say.

I jotted in my notebook: *busy as a day in the Old Testament.*

Then a moment of some tenderness. I saw Elizabeth Frame, unattended, walk over and sit next to Peter Lear, who was on the floor clutching his knees. She embraced him and even kissed the top of his head. Of course, I couldn't hear what she said, nor what he said back, but it had to qualify as urgent language. I watched this for a moment. I wanted to construct a memory of it. Peter looked to be hanging on for dear life.

Elizabeth stroked his hair. Suddenly Peter clamped his hands over his ears. Elizabeth tried to pry one of Peter's hands free but failed. *Cradled in the arms of a murderess, the stenographer rocked to and fro*—I realized I'd just captioned the moment; it's how I naturally think.

Mr. Solton along with Bevel Cousins swooped in and forcibly lifted Elizabeth to her feet and pulled her along toward the kitchen door. She was flailing away at them, crying out in protest. The only words I could make out were, "You cowards—he was a soldier!" Magistrate Spencer followed them close behind as they disappeared into the kitchen.

There are missed opportunities to be a better person. To dignify an undignified situation. You miss one of these, it doesn't come back. Sitting at my desk now, a glass of whiskey in hand, I ask myself, Should I have stayed with Peter Lear? I could see he was in a bad way. There was no doubt in my mind, the explosion had put him back in the trenches. The explosion had arrived from Passchendaele, traveled up his spine, percussed and echoed in his brain. I had read about shell shock. In my own paper the *Evening Mail*, I had read an amputee veteran of the Somme's account of it. My wife had seen a lot of it. She had described it in her letters. But until yesterday afternoon, I personally had never witnessed it. And I regret not having stayed with Peter Lear. Instead, I went to the wharf.

Outside, as I followed the crowd, I recognized Dr. Particulate and quickly caught up with him.

I gave him my bona fides and said, "Sir, the stenographer Peter Lear is under a desk. I think he's suffering shell shock. Can you take a look at him?"

"That'd be up to his physician in the city," Particulate said.

"But he's not in the city, is he? He's right here in Parrsboro. That explosion pretty much knocked him to the ground."

"I'm full up with appointments all day. I'll try to look in on Mr. Lear tonight. If I can. I know where he's staying."

"Hippocratic oath mean anything to you?"

"It will mean something to his physician in Halifax. Now, if you're done insulting me, I have to see if any local citizen is injured, you see." He turned and walked down to the wharf. After all, I'd asked him to do what I didn't do: attend to Peter Lear.

The wharf was dramatically astrewn. The first thing I noticed: whale-spattered people. Whale-spattered pilings. Floating chunks of whale in the shallows. Some of the pilings had been impaled by shards of skull and ribs, it looked like. There was half a dead horse sprawled on the beach, its guts spilled out like putrid kelp. Everywhere you looked were gulls. I walked up to Petrus Dollard. He looked shaken.

"I'm not being a newspaperman now," I said. "What the hell happened here?"

"There's a boy dead—Samuel Keegan. Sammy. His two elder brothers were killed in shelling at Vimy Ridge. Mary and Clement now have all their children completely disappeared. Completely missing from the earth. The world's turned upside down— parents getting orphaned by their children. See, crouched close together Hubbard was giving Sammy some know-how. Taking Sammy through the setting of the charges. Sammy walked off, but suddenly turned around. Then kaboom!"

I made a display of tucking my notebook in my back pocket. "Anyone else killed?" I said.

"Not that I know of. But there's others injured. Let's step

off to the side here." Actually, we climbed up onto the seat of a horseless buggy. "This is Mettie Bricknel's buggy. I imagine the explosion so badly spooked her horse that she unreined it and led it somewhere. Or Mettie might've just let the horse run. That dead horse isn't hers. Anyway, she won't mind if we sit here."

SOME HOURS LATER, I went to retrieve a wire Josephine said was from my wife. "You'll never guess what," Josephine said. "The revolver did hurtle right into the cabin of the *D. R. Kimber's Weeping Mermaid*. That boat took some considerable damage, too. But the revolver was there. Donald Kimber himself found it."

I sit here in my room. I sip my glass of whiskey. I read the wire that my beloved wife Amelia sent:

```
I AM CHANGED STOP I ADORE YOU AS ALWAYS BUT I AM
CHANGED STOP BY ALL I HAVE SEEN STOP I AM SENDING
THIS FROM HALIFAX STOP I AM HOME STOP ALBANIE
MUSGRAVE SAID WHERE YOU ARE STOP THE ATLANTIC
CROSSING WAS HELL STOP OUR HOUSE IS HEAVEN
STOP BUT BED EMPTY STOP LOVE AND KISSES STOP
YOUR AMELIA
```

When just an hour ago I had dozed off, I had a most ghastly nightmare. It was, I think, born of that word Josephine Huntley used, "hurtle." In a nightmare a single word can make for odd associations. At least that has been my experience. I don't need Sigmund Freud to tell me this. In my nightmare, one explosion connected to another. As everyone in the Western world—or at least Canada—knows, last December 6 was the Great Halifax Explosion, as it quickly came to be called. It happened at 9:05

a.m. Halifax Harbor was bustling with ships carrying troops, relief supplies, and munitions, all to be sent across the Atlantic. That morning, a Norwegian vessel, *Imo*, was arriving from New York City. At the same time, the rusting French tramp steamer *Mont Blanc* was forging through the narrows to join a military convoy that would escort it to Europe. The *Mont Blanc*'s cargo holds were packed with highly explosive munitions—two hundred tons of TNT, twenty-three hundred tons of picric acid, ten tons of gun cotton. As newspapers reported, somewhere around 8:45 a.m., in Halifax Harbor, the two ships collided and the first thing that happened was that the picric acid was set ablaze. The *Mont Blanc* veered toward shore and the crew abandoned ship. The terrible thing was, hundreds of people just stood along the waterfront, taking in the spectacle. What happened next was, the harbor pier burst into flame. The Halifax Fire Department was getting its truck into position when the *Mont Blanc* exploded. In the end, more than eighteen hundred Haligonans were killed and about nine thousand were injured, and almost the entire north side of the city was brought to wreckage, including over fifteen hundred homes. Statistics statistics statistics. Eight blocks up from the wharf, the front of the *Evening Mail*'s building was violently pocked by metal of some sort, hurtled all that distance from the *Mont Blanc*.

I mean, this was just last year!

Anyway, at the time, Amelia and I had an apartment in a brick building at 389 Argyle Street. When the explosion occurred, we'd been having a cup of coffee together in our small kitchen. I still had my pajamas on, but Amelia, dressed in slacks and a sweater but barefooted, had been up quite early, going through paperwork on some of her patients. The window overlooking the street suddenly shattered and we were hurtled all the way across our apartment and slammed against the wall. I was knocked unconscious, whereas Amelia's right shoulder had cushioned the blow, as it were, but her right wrist was badly sprained. She wouldn't perform surgery again for two full months. "And just when the city needs a surgeon most," she said. But thank God she'd maintained full consciousness, and when I came to, she was pressing a cold compress to my forehead. "I don't think it'll be possible to get you to hospital just now, darling," she said. Past headaches and dizziness for a couple of days, no real damage was inflicted. Amelia checked and rechecked. One night we were sitting in the kitchen again. The shattered window was boarded up. She said, "Dizziness gone?" I nodded yes. "Don't ever tell anyone I made a house call," she said. "If word gets out, I'll never hear the end of it."

But returning to the explosion right here in Parrsboro. As for the demolitionist Mr. Hubbard—there was no sign of him. None at all. After surveying the wharf and talking awhile with Petrus Dollard, I'd hurried up to Ottawa House and sent a wire to Albanie Musgrave, telling her about the whale and demolitionist and the immediate aftermath, et cetera—and I said that the Halifax police should locate Mr. Hubbard's family, if he had one. Back at the wharf, then, I learned that someone had found one of Sammy Keegan's shoes all the way up near Ottawa House. I spoke to the fellow who found it, Bernard Evers, who said he worked in lumber. "I only found the shoe. I didn't know whose it was. How could a shoe still be intact like that? Like Samuel just took it off and flung it himself. Some people brought a wooden table down to the beach, and different items—you know, things found along the beach or floating in the water—were set out on it. That's where I put the shoe. That's where Mary Keegan recognized it as her son's, God help her."

I had spent the next hour or so at the wharf. But I was all regret that I'd sent Albanie a wire. How could I write about Samuel Keegan? What did I know about that young boy's life? Nothing.

One thing that particularly struck me, though, was that at the wharf I saw Mr. Solton, Mr. Astoria, and Mr. Brewster. Obviously they had curiosities like anyone else, what's all the hubbub. But it meant that no one was guarding Elizabeth Frame—and my next thought was, how absurd in the first place, to have three burly men guarding Elizabeth under house arrest not two hundred meters from the house she was born and raised in.

I sidled up near to the three men. Actually, there would have been no reason for them to have recognized me or known my profession. They were holding some kind of confab. I only caught snippets: "This is the worst goddamn most tedious job I've ever . . ." and "Why not let's just take what's on offer and slip out of town . . ." and "The hearing's a farce." Collate these snippets together, and you certainly in the least had their attitude. But what stayed with me was, "Why not let's just take what's on offer . . ." What could that possibly mean? I thought, Well, maybe they've been offered a better-paying job elsewhere.

In fact, no sleep tonight. I can already tell that there will be no sleep tonight for me. Maybe I'll take a walk. In the village, not along the beach. I've got to be packed and ready at 5 a.m., as I've arranged passage to Halifax on the mail boat named *Neptune's Sad Sweetheart*. The mail boat's pilot, Odeon Forbisher, is in room 106 for the night.

ON THE LAM

Journal entry May 1, 1918. 4 a.m. Halifax

"Elizabeth and Peter Flee in the Night"
"Unsavory Chaperones"
"Neptune's Sad Sweetheart"
"A Favor Asked of Magistrate Spencer"

AS *NEPTUNE'S SAD SWEETHEART* SET OUT AT 5:30 yesterday morning, the sea was calm. A few wispy clouds, generally a rosy dawn. Acoustics-wise the Bay of Fundy was ventriloqual—the chugging of the engine sounded like it was coming from about a hundred meters south. A cormorant like a sentry on each buoy. Seagulls were all over the beach. Especially with that horse, the gulls continued their gruesome cleanup. *D. R. Kimber's Weeping Mermaid* was still anchored in harbor, but planks from its hull or whatnot bobbed and drifted here and there. On the beach, a scrap wood fire plumed white smoke. There were a dozen or so citizens milling about, and a few dogs. A little girl about age ten waved and Odeon Forbisher blasted two notes on his airhorn.

I hadn't any reason to think that Magistrate Spencer was going to be on the mail boat; why would he be, what with the hearing. I was on board because my wife had returned home, so too bad for the *Evening Mail*. As for any professional consequences, so be it. Anyway, there Magistrate Spencer was. I found myself standing next to him at the rail.

"You're Havenshaw, the reporter, right?" he said.

"That's right."

"I've read you. On occasion with interest."

"Quite surprised you're on this mail boat. What about today's hearing?"

"Both Elizabeth Frame and Peter Lear are on the lam. And I mean together."

"That's impossible."

"Not only is it possible, sir. It's a fact."

"Who allowed that to happen?"

Spencer stared out to sea. "Mr. Havenshaw, do you agree that people are capable of saying anything to anybody?"

"In my experience, yes."

"Well, this morning at about four a.m., I was again reading Oscar Asch's letters when there was a knock on my door. My uninvited guests were Mr. Solton, Mr. Astoria, and Mr. Brewster."

"Elizabeth Frame's chaperones."

"The same. With Mr. Solton being the spokesperson. He told me the mother, Elsbeth Frame, had approached them with money. Her life savings, Solton said. In a burlap sack."

"He was directly admitting to a magistrate he'd taken a bribe?"

"Dishonest man speaking honestly, or something like that."

"So the chaperones, what? Just looked the other way?"

"According to Mr. Solton, Elizabeth's mother had packed sandwiches. She went to her daughter's room. Mr. Lear was there. Toward Lear Elizabeth apparently had designs and was persuasive. The mother had arranged for a horse-and-buggy. As it turned out, by the time Solton knocked on my door, Elizabeth and Peter were a good five hours on the lam. Then Solton said he and the two others were going on to find work in Montreal."

"Can't you stop them?"

"What they did, it's actionable aiding and abetting, I suppose, but what good would come of that, say, that I ordered the

Northwest Mounted Police to arrest those sleazy journeymen? None as far as I can see. The better objective is Mr. Oscar Asch. My guess is that Elizabeth will eventually try to meet up with her original husband. At present, that's my working theory, anyway."

"What about Peter Lear?"

"Besotted with Miss Frame. I think besotted."

"So quickly, though."

"What goes into that might be forever his secret. All I know is he acted on it."

"I've just now remembered something. When I went to Peter Lear's room. This was after the first day of the hearing. He said, 'Elizabeth's quite pretty, don't you think?' "

"A wounded young man. Slightly hobbled. Newly employed. Impressionable, perhaps. Full of heartsick longings, perhaps. Did you notice what he did when the explosion occurred?"

"Flew right under the table."

"That had to be from the war."

"He was at Passchendaele."

"And you saw Miss Frame offering him ministrations?"

"I did see that."

"I suspect that was her opportune moment. I suspect she offered an invitation."

"My God, you think less of humankind than even me."

"Look, I don't know what's true and what isn't true here. I do know Elizabeth Frame exhibited the most impressive native intelligence I've ever seen. Actually, I've grown to admire her, in a way. She's original. Mind you, I'm not saying murder recommends her originality. But how many truly original people do you yourself know, Mr. Havenshaw? I've met a lot of very intelligent and accomplished people in my social circle, for instance.

But not necessarily *original*. I'd guess Miss Frame's appetites for life surprised even her. But if you quote my admiration in your newspaper, I'll sue your newspaper to kingdom come. I'll come after you in particular."

"So dead of night, off in a horse-and-buggy they went."

"That seems pretty much it."

"All of a sudden I fear for Peter Lear."

"Well, he wants something and she wants something. It'll either turn out to be the same thing or it won't."

"What's your best guess?"

"It won't."

Magistrate Spencer then reached into his suit-coat pocket and produced the revolver. He turned it over in his hand and laid it on the open palm of his other hand.

"I'm going to dine out on this object for a good long time," he said. "I've absconded with evidence. This little souvenir of the most eccentric legal proceeding of my career. Thus far."

We both looked out over the water for a while.

"Set aside why the hell Elizabeth married Everett Dewis in the first place," I said, "my question is, why do you think she murdered him? The actual why of it. In that exact moment, the why of it. I've been racking my brain."

"Any conjecture?"

"Maybe 'crime of passion.'"

"As for crime of passion, let me cite Nova Scotian law. 'Culpable homicide that otherwise would be murder may be reduced to manslaughter if the person who commits it did so in the heat of passion caused by sudden provocation.'"

"What about the whale? I imagine the whale itself had some powerful effect on Elizabeth."

"You're suggesting a mystical provocation."

"I suppose I am."

Spencer took this in and nodded. "Despite appearances, I'm not all linear, Mr. Havenshaw. My mind doesn't only trace a straight line. Perhaps Everett Dewis should just have gone to the window."

"Simple as that?"

"His wife was standing unclad in the moonlight. Good Lord, man. Just get up out of bed and go to the window."

It was the return run for *Neptune's Sad Sweetheart*—the mail boat would then navigate along the jigsaw coastline, south Atlantic shore, make eleven more stops, to pick up letters and packages bound for Halifax from the various outports. Odeon Forbisher called down from the wheelhouse, "Weather looks clear for the next ten minutes. For the Bay of Fundy, that's a bold prediction."

"Mr. Forbisher's entertaining," Magistrate Spencer said. "He delivered me to Parrsboro a week ago, so I could make preparations."

"Look," I said, "I get that we're strange bedfellows on this boat. And this is a top-notch request, and I've got no right or expectation in the matter. But might you keep me apprised? Apprised of Peter Lear and Elizabeth Frame. Details or generalities or anything. I don't live but five blocks from the courthouse."

"Let me start right now. Mr. Lear's also taken the stenographic machine with him."

"The machine's his property. It came out of his wages, remember?"

"Though what's so far recorded on it is property of the court. As for future employment, he's unlikely to garnish a letter of recommendation from me." I thought that sort of understatement almost an erasure. "Curious, though, his taking the machine on the lam. He must've had his reasons."

PILLOW TALK

Journal entry May 8, 1918. 4:45 a.m. Halifax

"In Bed Together"
"The Naval Demolitionist's Widow"
"Back to the Site of the Whale"
"First Stenographic Transcript from Peter Lear"

A PACKAGE, POSTED FROM SOMEWHERE IN THE province, arrived for me at the *Evening Mail*. It contained a transcript of Elizabeth Frame's words. Obviously, Peter Lear was the stenographer. What Elizabeth says in the transcript surprised the hell out of me. I'll get back to that in a moment.

~

I'M PRESENTLY SITTING, middle of the night, at the kitchen table in our small house at 2138 London Street, again writing in my journal. Thinking back on it, once I had debarked from *Neptune's Sad Sweetheart* and made my way home, it was just after midnight. Amelia and I had a long embrace. We stepped back to look at each other, then fell into exhausted laughter. The familiar laughter of thirteen years of marriage. Age thirty-seven, Amelia is a year older than me. I saw right away that Amelia had lost a little weight; the crow's-feet at both her eyes were more pronounced. But in our reunion moment, which was by candlelight as there was a blackout, I saw all her stalwart spirit and loveliness; her smile, as the saying goes, defuses the argument before the argument begins. She'd neatly ironed slacks and a silk blouse for the occasion, and, rare thing, had put on lipstick, a pale shade of red. "My husband at last," she said. "But you look a windblown fright." At unpredictable moments, in certain words or clusters of words, her Scottish childhood can be heard. It was heard in "windblown fright."

Then, in a dramatic and comical gesture, she took the stethoscope from her ever-present doctor's bag and placed it against my chest, listened, and said, "Good, you're alive. For months I've been among the dead and the living. Believe me, sometimes it was difficult to tell which was which." She listened through the stethoscope again. "I'd say you have fifty years left. Use your time wisely, especially tonight."

"First I need a bath."

"Miracles never cease. I'll sit and watch. We can talk."

"We're getting along very well, aren't we?"

"Not as good as we'll be getting along later."

"You look more beautiful than ever."

"Thank you, darling. But the medical work over there, and little sleep. Constantly fraught. Not a single peaceful hour. Not really. What it all took out of me. I'm afraid none of it refined my looks. These gray hairs arrived out of nowhere. And me in the prime of youth! Also, that my hair's cut so short to avoid lice."

"Let it grow out or don't. It's up to you."

"You worried about me day and night, didn't you?"

"You were gone one hundred fifty-nine days."

"My oh my. You counted."

"How was your health during? You might've purposely not wanted to worry me in your letters."

"Considering where our hospital tents were in relationship to the front, I was more concerned about Spanish flu than artillery. Though weeks on end, there was shelling heard day and night."

"Which reminds me, thank you for your letters. They kept you close. I don't know how you even found the time."

"Letters let me organize my emotions, Toby. You can understand that, right?"

"I was grateful they somehow got through."

I took off my clothes and put them in the hamper. Once I'd run a bath and eased down into it, taken up the scrub brush and soap, Amelia sat in a kitchen chair she'd set in the doorway. The light was still from the candles on the kitchen table.

"And speaking of my letters," she said. "Apart from what I described in them, did you notice anything unusual?"

"The handwriting itself."

"I've always prided myself on my flowing cursive, you know. Even my finicky aunt Eibhlín in Edinburgh used to ask me to take dictation for letters she wrote. Oh my goodness, did I ever get educated in what might be said in an adult letter. I was just nine or ten at the time."

"I noticed right away on the front of the first envelope to arrive. All cramped and spidery, right?"

"It was the strangest thing. After my first week of surgeries—night and day—I developed what they nicknamed 'scalpel tremors.' My wrists hurt like the devil and my hands shook and would cramp, even knot up—I had to put them in ice, when we had ice. All us field surgeons had to have our hands massaged—by the nurses, mainly. Sometimes we asked this or that soldier. They'd knead our hands front and back. So when I'd sit to write you a letter, I bent over the page and had to bear down on each *a, b,* or *c.* Some nights I felt like a Benedictine monk from the Middle Ages. I bet those monks were very skillful at massaging each other's hands."

Amelia went into the kitchen and brought back two glasses and a bottle of ginger-flavored brandy; I sipped mine while in the bathtub, she sipped hers back in the chair.

"I've brought authentic French perfume back from France—I've dabbed it on my wrists and the backs of my knees," she said. "Plus one other place."

Once out of the bath, I toweled off, and we took our reunion directly to the bedroom; let's just say I located all the perfume and the night was a reprieve from all ghastly things. Later, there was pillow talk—Amelia's always felt a marriage bereft of pillow talk isn't fully a marriage.

We lay entwined, bedclothes awry. Amelia said, "I imagine you want to know what I meant by 'I've changed.' You remember. In the wire I sent you. When I'd only just arrived home."

"Of course I remember. It was just yesterday, after all."

"But how could I not change? In the war, it was all camaraderie and nightmare—and all of it deepened my sense of purpose as a surgeon. So that's change right there. But it also changed me much for the worse. In terms of . . . *faith*. Not a word oft-used by me, is it, darling? I just lost whatever faith I had. The words that come to mind are: *The human capacity for cruelty.* Is this philosophical drivel? Probably it is."

"Not in the least."

"Here in Halifax, I've participated in surgeries of every stripe and from every violent cause. And you've heard it all, Toby. But what I saw in France, there was this one fellow, stretchered in in the middle of the night—eighteen, nineteen, possibly twenty at the oldest, name was Creighton McBurnie, he was from Tatamagouche, Nova Scotia—the sweetest face, but the body mangled. Just all torn up—" Amelia suddenly looked utterly lost. "Oh God, look at what I've brought to our pillow talk. Is our pillow talk now going to be all the world's despair?"

"If it has to be—at least for a while."

And almost immediately Amelia nodded off.

In a while, she disentangled from me in her sleep. Then I got up to make a coffee and write in this journal. I even made a few notes, inspired by Amelia's idea from some months ago, toward my writing a book about insomnia—or sleeplessness. "I can bring some good source material," she'd said. "You know, from nighttime at the hospital." She would bring up this project quite often and finally I became intrigued. I never thought I had a book in me, but she did. We'd had one lengthy conversation about it, during which she insisted that if I was going to write such a book, I should begin with my childhood. Because I'd told her that around age five or six, I started to have sleepless nights and had to figure out how not be afraid of that. This of course was right here in Halifax, where I was born and raised. My father ran a housepainting business; he had two employees. My mother was a manifest clerk for the Cunard Line, in their office at Pier 20. I was their only child. Generally speaking, our family life was solid and peaceful, as it regarded the three of us. I always felt my parents liked being with each other. They were both deep sleepers. Of course, the thing about insomnia is that you have to learn to make good use of it. You can't just be in some sort of catatonic state, or start talking to yourself, i.e., *I can't sleep, I can't sleep, I can't sleep.* Pulling your hair out. Becoming prayerful, just in order to ask God, What's wrong with me? It was a big and scary secret at first, which I felt I couldn't share with anyone. And from the start I could pretty much tell by eight or nine o'clock at night if I was going to be delivered up to a sleepless night. It was just something that registered in my body first. And then at a certain point, I'd realize, It's here again.

But on the above-mentioned night of Amelia's and my

reunion, after she'd been asleep for about an hour, she suffered what to my mind was her own version of shell shock. It came on like gangbusters. She more or less choked out, "Creighton Creighton Creighton—morphine—I can try to make you comfortable with morphine." She sat up but remained asleep; she threw her hands over her face and said, "No! No! No!—no ice cream just yet! Once you die I'll get you an ice cream." Then came a high-pitched, almost screamed sentence that contained German, French, and English words, all three obviously necessary to the conveyance of dread, but I couldn't make any sense of it. She took great gulps of air. When I sat on the bed and reached out and touched her face and said, "Amelia," she shoved me quite violently, "Back back back back, sir—you're contagious!"

Something like this has happened several times since Amelia's come home. I've told her about it in detail, as I knew she'd want and expect me to. "I've considered working just nights for a while," she said. "Just to give you some peace and quiet. But then I figured that Creighton McBurnie would just as easily find me sleeping daylight hours, too."

And just last night, Amelia brought the bottle of brandy to bed, along with a manila envelope. "I opened this," she said. "Though it was addressed to you."

It was the photograph of the whale that had been taken by Victor Alt.

"It's from what you told me about what happened in Parrsboro," she said. "It's the very whale, isn't it?"

Because I'd told her some about Elizabeth and Peter, and even Magistrate Spencer. I showed her the one-column piece in the *Evening Mail*. I told her about the death of little Samuel Keegan. I told her about the demolitionist Elliot Hubbard.

"That's really something," she had said. "A lot to take in, but I want to take it in—the one murder in Parrsboro, whereas I was surrounded by—if you will, if you will, if you will—thousands of murders. And now there's this murderer Elizabeth Frame loose in the province." I said that Magistrate Spencer was keeping me apprised. "At least you weren't sent with the NMP to find her. At least Albanie Musgrave—and you know there's no love lost between me and her—at least she's not putting you in harm's way."

"Anyway, it won't end well for Miss Frame."

"About the photograph . . ."

"The photographer, Victor Alt, announced he was selling copies. That was on the morning before the whale's obliteration. Something about the whale got to me. I don't know entirely what. I sometimes dream about it. And now, as it turns out, a thing has happened—at the newspaper."

"Just tell me."

"Albanie Musgrave wants a follow-up sort of piece—about the blowing up of the whale."

"What on earth for?"

"She's got her nose to the wind and her hackles up about the demolitionist, Mr. Elliot Hubbard."

"But you're with the crime page."

"Well, apparently Albanie's talked to the police. The police spoke to Hubbard's widow in Yarmouth. And there's some theory at work that Mr. Hubbard's death was actually a suicide. Which to Albanie falls under my purview, in her opinion. She is my boss, after all."

"My goodness. Albanie thinks this Mr. Hubbard blew himself up on purpose?"

"That's all I know so far."

"What legal category would that make that poor little boy Sammy Keegan?"

"I have to consult with Magistrate Spencer about that."

"What's first for you, then?"

"I have to interview the widow. She'll be brought in from Yarmouth. I think she packs herring there. Then I might have to return to Parrsboro. But just for an overnight at most."

"Is there any way out of this assignment?"

"Albanie feels I've already built up a little rapport in Parrsboro. I don't feel I have any at all. If I have to go, why not come with me?"

"I've got surgeries scheduled out for three weeks."

AND SO, LATE ON A RAINY MORNING, I met the demolitionist's widow, Martha Hubbard, at the Haliburton House Inn restaurant. The *Evening Mail* had arranged a room for her the previous night. And she'd spend a second night, and then be returned to Yarmouth. We met in the dining room, which was closed until dinner hour. Martha Hubbard was accompanied by her son, wearing his rain slicker and galoshes. At a corner table, he was playing both sides of a game of checkers. As I approached, I could see that Martha was about thirty years old, at most.

She was dressed entirely in black, a mourner's full regalia to be sure, including a black bonnet. She certainly cut a grievous figure; I didn't know for whose benefit.

When I said, "I'm Toby Havenshaw," she gestured for me to sit down across from her. When I sat, she said, "Thank you for meeting with me. Albanie Musgrave, your superior, has paid me thirty dollars."

"It wasn't necessary to mention that."

"It was for me."

"Despite your troubles, you traveled all this way." I placed my notebook and pencil on the table.

Of Martha Hubbard, everything struck a formal tone, and I fell right into place. She seemed comfortable with this. Martha Hubbard was drinking a cup of tea. Her son had a glass of orange juice set next to the checkerboard. When she removed her bonnet, I saw that she had tightly curled straw-colored hair, pale skin, almost alabaster, an oval face, like you'd maybe see in a Victorian pendant, except her forehead had deep worry lines, as if marking the latitude of her sorrow.

"I think this inn has some foreigners on staff," she said.

"My wife and I have dinner here once or twice a year."

"Nobody German, as far as I can tell, though. If there was a German cleaning my room, I'd ask the police for another place to stay."

"I understand that your husband served. He distinguished himself."

"Physically he came back unwounded and whole. Mentally Elliot was what they call 'bifurcated.' It was like his mind had a dual citizenship—home in Yarmouth, but also still in the trenches in France. My dear husband became bifurcated."

"Is your son bearing up?"

"My boy sitting right over there, his name is Elliot Jr. He's ten. He wears his father's two war medals night and day. And I mean on his nightshirt. What's more, he's got to blowing up tin cans with firecrackers. He's got into his father's stash, including Roman candles and Catherine wheels. I've put the kibash on that. But you can't stop the inherited inclination, now, can you."

Silence for a moment. "I must ask, Mrs. Hubbard, why did you agree to speak with the *Evening Mail*?"

"The reason is quite simple. I consider my husband a murderer."

"You mean of Samuel Keegan, the little boy."

"I mean Samuel Keegan, exactly. I consider my husband his murderer."

I was simply gobsmacked. I looked over and saw Elliot Jr. do a triple jump, thus exploiting the advantage he'd provided against himself. I got a brief glimpse of his father's medals under his slightly open rain slicker.

"Cat got your tongue?" Martha Hubbard said.

"That's one way to put it. Can you kindly explain."

"Not kindly, but I can explain." She reached into her handbag and took out a folded piece of paper, which she handed to me. It was in cursive that resembled barbed wire, barely legible:

My loving wife Martha,

I'm hired as you know to dispatch with dynamite a beached whale in Parrsboro outport. There was enough confidence in my skills that I was paid half in advance, which sum is deposited in our bank. I love you and I love our dear boy Elliot Jr. But since France my mind is all bad weather. I cannot live inside this weather any longer. Sleep is fugitive at best if it even arrives. Please go live with my sister Mary in Gabarouse as she can help

raise Elliot Jr. It would benefit everyone. I am sorry. I am sorry,
but I will be leaving this earthly paradise with the whale.

Your husband Elliot

When I went to hand back the note, Martha said, "I suggest you copy it out in that notebook of yours because I'm eventually going to burn this one." So I did that.

"Why did you show this to me?" I said.

"Because I want you to confess on my deceased husband's behalf. Please put his note in your newspaper."

"It might cause great pain to the family of Samuel Keegan."

"Don't you dare judge me."

"And what about your own son? It might risk his shame and humiliation, eventually."

"I'm going to change our last name. Plus which, I intend to move to New Zealand. I have a cousin there. Our church will help with expenses."

"Is this some attempt at redemption, Mrs. Hubbard?"

"Call it what you want. It's not easy for me to ask a favor."

"It's not a comfortable favor for me to be asked. I'll give it some serious thought, though. I'm sorry you've been widowed."

"I don't need your pity."

"Why show the note to anyone? Why not keep it private?"

It was clear that this was not the kind of conversation Martha Hubbard had anticipated or wanted, and now she'd had quite enough. She tore the page from my own notebook, stuffed it into my hand, clenched my fingers into a fist and held it fast. I could see her forcing back tears. She let go of my hand. She stood up from the table, and I stood up.

Elliot Jr. called out, "Mister, come here please!" I walked over to his table. He pointed at the checkerboard. There were about ten pieces still in play. "Your move," he said. "You're red."

I obediently studied the board. I moved a red piece. Elliot Jr. clapped his hands together and said, "My prayer was just answered!" He double-jumped me.

His mother said, "Elliot Jr., we're going up to our room now."

Elliot Jr. looked at me and said, "My father could beat you blindfolded at checkers."

He placed the pieces and the board in a leather case. His mother took his hand in hers, and they walked out of the dining room. I thought, There goes a family that's half orphaned, if you reconfigure the definition the way Petrus Dollard had.

That evening I told Amelia about my time with Martha Hubbard and that I was leaving the next morning for Parrsboro. "I'll be in surgery at six a.m." she had said. "Do you want me to wake you?"

"Yes, we can at least have a quick coffee together."

The next morning, when Amelia went to the hospital, I drove one of the *Evening Mail*'s touring cars to Truro, then west to Parrsboro, my quite recent haunt. It took all of the morning and into early afternoon. I set up in Gillespie House Inn, this time in room 208. The inn was open for business again. In my room, I had a lamb and mustard sandwich for dinner and reviewed my notes.

On the following morning I had a coffee and scone at Harbor Bakery, where I felt neither welcomed nor neglected. When it comes to human discourse, such blatant, perfectly calibrated civility can be unnerving, I've always found. Going here and there in the village, I did manage that day to fill two small notebooks with references and opinions about the actions of Elliot Hubbard. Rector Shrevard said, "The Keegan family directly requested I not forgive him in a sermon, and I said the thought never crossed my mind. Which it hadn't and won't ever."

Two nights there was quite enough. Formerly in my journal I wrote that I'd be very uncomfortable writing about the death of Samuel Keegan. And now, professional assignment or not, I still felt uncomfortable. But oddly enough, it was a conversation with Josephine Huntley, early on the morning of my departure, in her office at Ottawa House, that put me a little more at ease with this. The thing I had to start admitting to myself was that the events in Parrsboro were changing me. I didn't have any clarity about it; it was more an incipient feeling, like insomnia marshaling its forces on any given night since I was five or six years old, something like that.

Josephine and I had tea together. "Get that sheepish look off your face," she said. "And stop staring at the floor. It wasn't your fault what happened with that demolitionist. Nobody's going to put a dunce cap on you and make you stand in the corner. We know what a newspaper reporter does for a living. Likewise, I don't need anyone's permission to convey my recollections or opinions, now, do I?"

She proceeded to describe Samuel Keegan's funeral. (Her phrase was, "sobbing near to break the church windows.") She told me about repairs made to D. R. Kimber's *Weeping Mermaid*. She told me about the church social that raised funds for Elsbeth Frame. ("An outsider might see that as charity toward the family of a miscreant, but yet and still, Lizzie was Elsbeth's very own daughter, wasn't she. Who can't understand a village helping out can't understand anything.") At the end of Josephine's lecture on local ethics, she reached into her desk drawer and took out a book and handed it to me. "The stenographer Peter Lear left this in his room. I highly doubt anyone in Parrsboro's going to see him again. But somehow I thought you might. Someday somehow." It was the collection of Heraclitus. Looking at it, I thought, Lear must have been in a real hurry, in the dark, to leave this sacred book behind. Yet he hadn't left his pocket diaries behind.

In terms of what pertinent information I'd received about the tragedy of Samuel Keegan, the standout was what Petrus Dollard told me.

"What I witnessed is burnt into my brain," he said. "You see, it started out that Mr. Hubbard had been giving a close-up lesson in setting charges to Sammy Keegan. That's how it looked to me. This went on a good fifteen minutes. I don't know how much technical know-how Sammy might've taken in, a boy that age, but it must've been exciting for him. He must've seen his schoolmates seeing he'd been favored as such. He just looked so delighted. Just delighted. Then a dark cloud fell across Mr. Hubbard's face, let's just say it was noticeable. From my close perch atop the pilings, let's just say it was noticeable.

"Mr. Hubbard then said something to Sammy, and Sammy broke into tears, and then Mr. Hubbard pushed Sammy away, and I mean hard. Sammy tumbled backward. He got to his feet and walked right up to Mr. Hubbard and took a swing at him. The swing ricocheted off Hubbard's shoulder. Brave boy, I'd call that. Mr. Hubbard then grabbed Sammy and tried to embrace him, but Sammy got out of his grip and walked off a ways. At which point Mr. Hubbard went back to his demolition. He'd already set charges along the whale. Sammy was behind Hubbard so Hubbard couldn't see, but Sammy then started to stomp back toward him full-fisted on both hands, tough little fellow. And that's when it happened. The whole beach exploded, it looked like."

To my mind this account didn't exactly exonerate Elliot Hubbard. After all, he'd recklessly invited Samuel Keegan in close to his work. But thanks to Petrus Dollard, I surmised that at least Hubbard had acted out of some conscious recognition, but he did so too late. I imagined no solace to the Keegan family in knowing any of this; I think none at all. (Rector Shrevard said, "With a situation like this, the Lord himself often can't offer comprehensive solace"—what an equivocating phrase, I thought. Who cares about "comprehensive"? Any solace would do.) Quite the résumé for Elliot Hubbard: all in his given life he blew up bridges in France and Belgium, blew up roads over there, and in Canada a whale, and a child. And now his son's wearing his medals. I'd change my last name, too, if I were his widow.

Driving back to Halifax, I decided the title I'd give my piece was "Tragedy in Parrsboro in the Death of a Child." I would keep Elliot Hubbard's dubious note of contrition out of it, I decided. I thought not to even mention it to Albanie Musgrave.

Amelia was exhausted from back-to-back surgeries when I got home. "I've got dinner from Haliburton House's kitchen," she said. "You must be famished. I'm famished." At the kitchen table, I told her about Parrsboro. "Oh, that reminds me," she said. "Magistrate Spencer wants to see you. He contacted you at the paper, and they contacted me at hospital. The man is persistent, isn't he?" Later, our clothes fell away. Later yet—and this felt so much the necessary absence of urgent language—we had pillow talk that didn't include the world outside of our bedroom.

⌒

IT'S NOW 4:45 A.M. I laugh thinking, suddenly, that my whole life since age five might become research for a book about sleeplessness. Just the odd thought there. In my journal I now will copy out the transcript that was sent to me at the *Evening Mail*. At a quick first reading, it was clear that Peter Lear intermittently had some responses, but those weren't allowed into the transcript itself.

I'm with child, Peter, as you know. But now that you and I have had amorous congress, I'll mark it up to loneliness, but also you're not half unattractive and you are risking things, as my travel companion. I made Magistrate Spencer cringe, didn't I, when I said I was impetuous. But you exercised none too little impetuousness yourself, didn't you, when my mother's horse-and-buggy arrived? Of course you'd just partaken of my seduction, hadn't you, sweet boy. We are on the lam now. There's no other way to look at it. And during this being on the lam, if we stop at a place for the night, I might have to mention I'm with child, and I might have to say you are the father, for appearances' sake. Though you don't have a wedding ring, do you? Let's see who notices and who doesn't, shall we? Anyway, the farther we travel out into the province, the less chance people will have knowledge of me and what I've done. My evil deed, you see.

Was I your first time? I thought as much. I noticed as much. How much money do we have left? I had better check. Anyway, where to go next, do you think? I've looked at the map, and think maybe Pictou. Look at you at your machine! Clack clack clack, but of course I asked you to take down my thoughts. But I'm going to speak directly about life, here. So clack away.

And here you are with me. Why are you here with me? Because you know I'm going to Oscar Asch. I haven't lied to you about that. Oscar, my one living husband. He's expecting me. But no, don't think I'm not grateful for you, otherwise I'd be alone. But it was rash and stupid, you were too easily persuaded. Maybe you gave up on your former life too easily. Rash behavior. You gave no mind to consequences. You may still salvage a life. I no longer can.

Maybe we should travel up to Cape Breton. What do you think? In the end, God will bathe one of us in his mercy. Come on, now, really, which one of us do you imagine that will be? You should leave. You should leave. Once the sandwiches were gone, I felt motherless. You don't know this, but at the bottom of my suitcase lies my wedding dress. Neatly folded.

All right, I'm just talking, so let me talk. I didn't have my full say at the hearing. I may have caused my mother a lot of pain. While Mother had never imposed her opinions about Everett Dewis, that did not mean I didn't know what they were. I gave in to wanting to give her a married daughter who lived right down the road. But I cannot blame anyone but myself. She would have seen Oscar as a foreigner. And he would never not live in the city.

But why on earth marry Everett in the first place? How godless and despairing a behavior toward Oscar in absentia, and when I told my mother I had accepted Everett's proposal of marriage, do you know what she said? She said, "Well, Lizzie, you grew up with him." That was really all she could manage. Yet it was true, I did grow up with Everett. And when he came back from France, as so few men from Parrsboro and neighboring outports did, we went for a few walks together along the beach and road, and we went out in a dinghy half a dozen times. He talked a lot about what he'd gone through. He was more in a hurry to live than before. That's how he put it: "I'm more in a hurry to live." And as for his declared love for me, I became persuaded within the confines of the walks and dinghy and local confinements. Some men might've come home from France or Belgium with more patience, I suppose, but not Everett, and he'd appraised me as someone he could hurry on in life with. I knew his intentions. My mother knew his intentions. One day Rector Shrevard came to tea to our house in order to sponsor Everett's intentions.

All the able-bodied local men were in marked graves in France, and a number of empty gravestones in Parrsboro had their names on them, too. People needed a grave to visit, and who ever could travel to France for that purpose? Girls I'd grown up with, some had already married. Theresa Candle— she married a fellow from Great Village. These decisions were all around me. For some these decisions seemed to be made easy as the sun coming up. I had a serious marriage talk with my mother—this is before I went to Halifax. She refused to be for or against Everett. "In marriage they say it's give-and-take," she said, 'but not everyone can meet the other halfway on things. Your father gave a lot, on certain days. Some men and women are capable of only reaching less than halfway." That sort of circumspection isn't too encouraging for a daughter, but it was my mother's nature. And a daughter might get so worn down, she starts to turn negatives into potential positives, or something like that. But then I signed up for the mail-order composition classes. Then Oscar Asch was delivered by mail boat to me.

And with the very first lesson, I was over the moon. It wasn't so much that I romantically read into Oscar's lesson, which was technically about music and music alone. Some people read words and others read into them. It was the letter itself, you see. Reading his letter put my heart on notice. It felt the way when at age twelve I'd read five Robert Louis Stevenson's books from the library in just two days. You burn more than one candle reading like that.

My response to Oscar's first letter obviously had nothing to do with his intentions as an instructor. I wrote a twelve-page letter in response, some of which had to do with music composition, but a lot didn't. Truth be told—and I was quite aware of this—with just that first letter, Everett Dewis fell away. Almost right away I began to actually imagine myself traveling for the first time to Halifax.

As Oscar's letters continued to arrive, I was using the church piano. Rector Shrevard knew of my mail-order lessons. I could already play quite well. Oscar's first few letters pretty much kept to how to write your own music, and for me such a daunting endeavor meant for me the need to please him. And it was entirely my doing when my letters got longer and longer, and I even pressed a fingerprint of perfume—perfume borrowed from Theresa Candle, already a married woman—pressed a fingerprint of perfume onto the salutation of one letter. Maybe tittering, maybe stupid, but at the same time deadly serious and hopeful, and I pressed the perfume without regret.

In my darkest hours since murdering Everett, I sometimes think what gathered forces on our wedding night in Ottawa

House, was all those books I'd read. I was grateful for every single book, too. Books are guides to travel out of a confining village life, you see—follow me, I'll take you elsewhere—and then you fall asleep reading, the book falls to the floor, and you wake up almost shocked to be back in your same old life. And one word I got from Robert Louis Stevenson that perfectly fit my life was "sequestered." You know—isolated. Hidden away. And I'd write that word over and over and over on a piece of paper, and then a romantic logic presided and I lied to my mother and went to Halifax.

I had arranged a room at the Seaview Rooming House on Gottingen Street, which didn't by the way have a view of the sea, though maybe it once had. It cost twenty cents per night. I had a nice clean room. There were lovely and exciting street noises out the window. Soldiers were at the pubs. Influenza was mentioned in the headlines, street-corner kiosks, all like that, newspapers and magazines. The 1917 explosion still very much everywhere in evidence. It was the first time I'd sat drinking coffee outdoors! Despite my restricted finances, I did that twice.

But the purpose of being in Halifax that I'd told my mother was to purchase a wedding dress.

But I had lied because it wasn't my sole purpose. Because to my mind I was about to have a rendezvous. I didn't yet know how Oscar thought of our meeting in person, either. I knew how I wanted him to feel about it. And when he appeared at the outdoor table, just a block from the rooming house, he cut a dashing figure, but older-looking than I'd imagined. He had an accent, no doubt acquired in Bavaria. And to top it all off, he'd brought me a present—a book—"Principles of Music Composition" by Arthur Sharpinsky and Olga Sharpinsky. And Oscar

had written on the title page: "To my pupil Elizabeth Frame
with intrigue and best wishes."

How do you spell "intrigue," you ask? I-N-T-R-I-G-U-E.

I'm not all that confident you can understand this, Peter,
but at that moment, in that café, on that warm spring day, my
having read Robert Louis Stevenson's books and sitting with
my dashing music composition instructor, Bavarian accent
included, I can't say why, but I just blurted out, "Have you ever
thought of traveling to Polynesia?" Oscar looked quite startled
but he then took a deep breath and said, "Not until this very
moment." I held on to my senses, though, though I knew what
was occurring, I had someone to talk with. So we talked about
music and books, simple as that, and look what's happened in a
few months: life's become all madness. Once back in Parrsboro,
Halifax became a dream, Parrsboro a nightmare, and in matrimonial terms I'd chosen both. God in heaven, listen to what
I've just said, listen to what I've just said.

I should be drowned like a kitten, stuff me into a burlap sack
and throw me into the ocean. Yet my firm belief is that now only
Oscar can save me—only he can get us to Polynesia. And it's not
just that I've always aimed my darkest imaginings directly at
myself, but that now I'm having dark imaginings about things
to come. But none of them so far have included Polynesia. Polynesia has only beautiful light.

The transcript ends there.

AWAKE ALL NIGHT WITH POLICE

Journal entry June 27, 1918. 4:10 a.m. Halifax

"Book on Sleeplessness?"
"Stakeout at 118 Kane Street"
"Notice of Petit-de-Grat"

WRITING THIS AT THE KITCHEN TABLE. AMELIA
is asleep. Yesterday morning at 10 a.m. I went to Magistrate
Spencer's office next to the courthouse on Spring Garden Road.

"I read your piece about the demolitionist," he said. "That
outport's cursed. But so is the world just now. What's that in the
envelope you're holding?"

I told him I'd received a transcript from Peter Lear, Elizabeth
Frame talking. I set the envelope on his desk. He gestured for me
to sit down in the chair opposite his desk, put on his spectacles,
and read the transcript while I sat there.

When he finished, he said, "May God judge me, but somehow this makes me even more curious about the workings of
Miss Frame's mind. Practically every one of her sentences con-
tains indirection. I wonder if she secretly writes poetry. I remember that on the mail boat you said you feared for Peter Lear. I
somehow fear for Elizabeth Frame. So between us they're both
feared for. 'Separate fools on the same fool's path.'"

"I was told at the police station that they interviewed
Oscar Asch."

"Yes, the police spoke in a small room with him."

"Spoke roughly with him, do you think?"

"It's normal procedure with anyone having anything to do
with the perpetrator."

"Normal procedure, of course."

"And since you've given me something to read and ponder, I'll return the favor." He reached into his desk drawer, took out a few pages, and handed them to me. "Breaking the rules here a little, but so be it. Keep these for your private file—just don't tell anyone how you got them. Besides, I have a copy."

He left his office for some reason or other. I read the pages. It was Spencer's official response to the police request for his "general impressions." It read as follows:

To put it in the simplest terms, legally speaking, Mr. Oscar Asch has done nothing I can find that is actionable. He has a legitimate mail-order music composition business. The whole former dustup, i.e., the Sedition Act, came to nothing. He was legally married to Elizabeth Frame. Furthermore, there is no evidence that he married in order to help with his ongoing petition for Canadian citizenship. Of course, he was informed by the police that his wife is a fugitive from justice. My understanding is that he was shown the "Wanted" poster. According to the police interrogator, Asch seemed ignorant of the murder in Parrsboro. ("For a man his age, he seemed the star-crossed newlywed"— Sergeant Brakeman, interlocutor) There were found in his apartment no recent letters from Elizabeth Frame—that is, since she's been on the lam. One might even conclude that Oscar Asch has managed to construct, within the confines of his immigrant status and strivings, a respectable life. The fact that Sergeant Brakeman considered it questionable, even dubious, that Asch took private cooking lessons from two different foreign chefs in Halifax, did not have any import for me. As for Elizabeth Frame: While she did something corrupt by marrying Mr. Everett Dewis, there still might be potential legal and time-consuming logjams, because Oscar Asch is a foreigner. My hope is that during his interrogation Asch was not crudely informed of the conflicting marriage of his wife to Mr. Everett Dewis. Question: Would the courts even uphold an indictment of polyandry against Frame? Who might even care? Why should the court waste its time on this? Cases are backed up like a sewer. Especially now that Everett Dewis is dead, the double marriage might, at best, possibly be seen as a confounding but finally dismissable anomaly. I would have to research the law here. On the other hand, the brutal murder committed by Elizabeth Frame needs to be followed closely and dealt with. It may be agreed that Mr. Peter Lear is in some sort of trouble here, though I cannot yet determine what kind. But Elizabeth Frame needs to stand trial for homicide. That is the central fact here. Bloodhounds are set loose in the province, and one trusts she will eventually be found. A prosecutor will stand up and say, "This woman shot her husband thrice and killed him, and she admitted as much."

When Spencer returned to his office, he said, "I know Oscar is waiting for his wife. We've got a twenty-four-hour watch."

"Anything new on Elizabeth and Peter?"

"Operatives seem to be chasing their tails. But then again, a war's on, my friend, and we're understaffed. No, no word on the sorry fugitives, I'm afraid. But a promise is a promise, so when I know, you'll know."

"Maybe she'll get to Polynesia."

"Dream on, Mr. Havenshaw. You know as well as I do, one way or the other, Elizabeth Frame will die on the lam or go to prison. One doesn't need a crystal ball."

"Well, you're a busy man." I started for the door. "Thanks for seeing me."

I went straight to the police station and asked Sergeant Rosset Harnes, a contact I'd had for at least ten years, if I could be on the stakeout of Oscar Asch's apartment that night. "It'd be the midnight to six a.m. shift," he said. He didn't seem to have much reluctance, actually. I suppose he did exactly as he pleased. "Be at the station here at eleven forty-five or we'll leave without you."

⁓

AFTER CLEARING DINNER PLATES, Amelia and I ate pieces of store-bought cherry pie for dessert, with vanilla ice cream. I'd already mentioned I'd be on the stakeout.

Amelia said, "I'm assisting in major surgery, also beginning at midnight. We're short-staffed."

"So breakfast together then?"

" 'Sleepless Man and Wife, Up All Night.' Why not make that the title of a chapter in your book on insomnia?"

"This may surprise you, but I've already taken some notes."

"It's a good idea, that book. I hope you write about when it started for you, sleepless nights, Toby. Childhood. It's important."

"So you believed me, what I said just now about taking notes."

"You said it, so I believed you. Look, you may have doubts whether you can write the thing. But your doubts aren't mine."

"It sounds like an arduous night ahead for you."

"Actually, I should try and get some sleep between now and then. Or just a lie-down. Then coffee at the hospital. One cup, for alertness."

We lay down side by side on our bed.

"You seem to have something particular on your mind," Amelia said. "If I'm wrong, I'm wrong."

"I think Albanie wants me off the crime page."

"Why, possibly?"

"I think she thinks—how did she put it. I've 'lost some objectivity.'"

"Does this have anything to do with your obsession with Parrsboro, do you think?"

"Well, clearly you think it does."

"The photograph of the whale is tacked above your desk at home here."

"Turns out I wasn't aware of something. That what I first handed in about the demolitionist, Albanie thought was a sprawling mess. She even accused me of being drunk when I wrote it, which I wasn't, needless to say. She assigned a rewrite. But when I read my original a few days later, I saw what she meant. All sorts of digressions and tributaries. And some real heart-on-your-sleeve lines such as, 'The outport of Parrsboro has suffered mightily from strange and disparate incidents.'"

"A bit poetical, but from what you told me, essentially true."

"Still, not no-frills journalism."

"Why not just wait and see what happens with Albanie?"

"She already assigned me—I can hardly say the words. A 'human interest story.' For God's sake, it could even end up in the Culture section."

"What's the piece about?"

"I'm to travel over to Petit-de-Grat, to write about a village already hit by Spanish flu. You know, the effects on daily life."

Amelia was quiet for a few moments. "Darling," she finally said, "might this be an opportunity? Part one might be the assignment itself, but part two might be a more personal opportunity. I'm just thinking out loud here."

"Opportunity for what?"

"We're in bed together here. Please put that irritable tone in your back pocket."

"Sorry."

"Opportunity to discover your writing skills might go beyond even what you're already so good at. I'd never cast aspersions on your crime stories, of course. They're top-flight, though by definition not uplifting. It sometimes concerns me, all those murders might be wearing you down, in some incipient way. I mean the very subject itself, though it's your expertise. And of course it's so far your professional reputation. I don't take any of that lightly."

"I really am slowly beginning to warm to the idea of a book. But I do need a paycheck."

"Let's drop it for now. We've both got long nights ahead. When do you go to Petit-de-Grat?"

"Not for months. I'd guess October. All sorts of arrangements have to be made."

"My concern is Spanish flu by then will have gotten worse. But there's no predicting, is there?"

"No, there isn't."

"What's in between now and then?"

"I'm to sit in this or that courtroom here in Halifax. Typing up summaries of court proceedings. You know, who's accused of what. Just think, here I've won prizes for my work with the *Evening Mail*, but I'm being treated like a cub reporter. Because I wrote a sentence influenced by Shakespeare?"

"It may be time for a sit-down with Albanie Musgrave. Have it out with her. Say, I just thought of something. Why not strangle her and then write a piece about it?"

"For now, here's how I'm looking at it. I intend on my own time to stay close as I can to Frame and Lear, as Magistrate Spencer says he'll keep me apprised. I need to keep thinking of it as a mystery unfolding. Abanie, allowing me only one column, meant it all became bottom-drawer for her. But it's top-drawer for me."

"Look, you could easily get work at another paper. You get flirted with every other month. What's that fellow's name, over at the *Herald*?"

"Homer Orlen. Top-flight editor. Though he's also written two very bad dime novels."

"He'd put you right on the crime page, if you still wanted that."

"There's no guarantee of that. But he has asked directly." We held hands. "I need to figure it out."

"In the meantime, here we are. Still very much in love and bills getting paid. Unlike most."

She closed her eyes but I could tell she couldn't sleep.

⌒

I WAS AT THE POLICE STATION at 11:45 sharp. Sergeant Rosset Harnes was waiting on the front step with a copper whom I was introduced to as Officer Philip Ridge, his nephew, who was only two years on the force.

"This will be my nephew's first stakeout," Harnes said. "Not your first, though, right, Havenshaw?"

"My third, actually."

"Quite the veteran," Harnes said. He took a tone with me.

"Thanks for letting me tag along."

We got into the police car, with Officer Ridge at the wheel.

"You and me, Havenshaw," Sergeant Harnes said, "have done give-and-take favors for each other for years. That's the world we choose to live in, right?"

I remained silent; it seemed a direction I wanted to avoid.

"Mr. Oscar Asch's apartment is 118 Kane," Harnes said. "Just up from the dockyards."

"I know the neighborhood," I said. "There was a murder at 176 Kane."

"When was that?" Harnes said.

"December nineteen, four years ago. Jasper Sydney Olson. Age forty-eight. The wife called it an accident."

"I remember it," Harnes said. "The son, Thomas, sixteen. Took a kitchen knife to his own father's heart while he was sleeping. The wife conveniently in the privy down the hall."

"Some accident," Officer Ridge said.

"Beatrice Olson claimed her son sleepwalked nightly," Harnes said.

"Were you in the courtroom?" I said.

"Just the one day," Harnes said. "When the defense brought in a sleepwalk expert."

"From Montreal," I said. "I remember that."

"Under a merciless cross-examination from prosecutor Orville Pale," Harnes said, "Mr. Expert Witness got all blushed and flustered. 'Possibly I didn't have enough time to study this case long enough.' Ha! He could've studied it till hell froze over. I liked the final words Pale said in his summation. 'Ladies and gentlemen, this murder was a planned thing.'"

"What a quack, that sleepwalk expert," I said.

"Remember his theory?" Harnes said. "He theorized that one out of every three people on a Montreal streetcar on any given day was sleepwalking. Remember what Pale said to that? He said, 'My educated guess is nobody's ever stepped from a Montreal streetcar with a knife in their heart.' No retort has to make perfect sense if it's said the right way."

"It brought the house down," I said. "Thomas Olson got thirty years."

"Headline in the *Evening Mail* was, 'Sleepwalk Defense Wakes Up Jurors to Say Guilty.' Which I personally thought was catchy."

We turned onto Kane Street and parked across from the run-down brick apartment building at 118. I had a thermos and offered coffee all around. No takers but myself. Harnes took out a pair of binoculars and cleaned the lenses.

"What are we looking for?" Officer Ridge said.

"Mr. Oscar Asch," Harnes said. He unfolded from his pocket three pieces of paper stapled together, and quoted, "'Age forty-three. Medium height. Medium build. Hair: black, combed straight back. Eyes: brown. Other features: neatly trimmed beard. Nationality: Bavaria.'"

"What's Bavaria?" Officer Ridge said.

Sergeant Harnes ran his finger down the second page. "Okay, this is complicated," he said. "It's all caught up with a revolution that's going on right now. The so-called People's State of Bavaria tried to replace the Kingdom of Bavaria. There's a certain Kurt

Eisner, who's called the minister president of the Free People's State of Bavaria. There was also the Bavarian Soviet Republic. Screw it—I'm just going to flunk this goddamn history lesson. What's it have to do with our stakeout, anyway? All I needed is what this Bavarian Oscar Asch looks like."

"I like history," Officer Ridge said. "I took a course at Dalhousie."

Sergeant Harnes tossed the paperwork at his nephew and said, "You take it, then. We're in Halifax, Nova Scotia, not the Free People's State of Bullshit. If Asch leaves his apartment, we follow him. If he doesn't leave, we sit here and see if his fugitive wife shows up. If she shows up, try not to get shot by her. Simple as that."

"Of all my three uncles, you're the most sophisticated," Officer Ridge said. He glanced through the paperwork. "Says right here that this Oscar Asch meets once a month with some sort of music discussion group."

"That could be a front," Harnes said. "It's all Europeans." Then in a moment Harnes added, "Put your homework away. The reason we're parked here in front of 118 Kane is that Elizabeth Frame is married to Oscar Asch. The very Elizabeth Frame wanted for homicide. Magistrate Spencer—and I'm in agreement—is convinced that she's on her way to Halifax."

"Pretty cut and dried," Officer Ridge said.

"It's not Bavarian politics, nephew," Harnes said. "It's a stakeout."

We said nothing for at least an hour. Just sat in the car surveying the street and the front door of the apartment building. Then the door opened. Out stepped Oscar Asch.

"It's two twenty-five a.m.," Harnes said. "Nephew, write that down." Officer Ridge jotted the time down in his notebook.

Asch was dressed in an elegant overcoat; underneath we could see he wore a suit and tie. "I firmly believe those are European shoes he's wearing," Harnes said.

Holding a tray, Oscar Asch crossed the street and walked directly to our car. Officer Ridge rolled down the window.

"I suppose there's no need to introduce myself," Oscar said, with a more than noticeable accent. "Oscar Asch, husband to Elizabeth Frame. Go upstairs if you choose. Search my apartment. My wife is not there."

"Write all that down," Harnes said to his nephew.

"Officers, I've been—how to say it? Cooking up a storm?" Oscar said. He nodded at the three bowls on the tray. An incredibly tantalizing aroma filled the car. "I've got food left from hosting my music appreciation group. It keeps well. I have brought paprika schnitzel, on the plate here. Next to it is called *Kartoffelkroketten*, which in English would be something like 'potato croquette.' Also here is *Zwiebelkuchen*—onion cake."

Oscar looked at Officer Ridge and said, "Did you serve in—" but Ridge interrupted and said, "If you're asking if I killed Germans, the answer is yes."

"I was asking if you served," Oscar said. "Please take a big piece of onion cake." And lo and behold, Officer Ridge reached out and took a piece.

Sergeant Harnes opened the passenger-side door and stepped out. He walked around the car and stood in front of Oscar Asch. I thought, This is not good, this is going to be bad.

Harnes took out his police revolver and placed the barrel end to Oscar's forehead. "I didn't serve in France or Belgium," he said, "but I wouldn't mind serving right here on Kane Street in Canada."

It was impressive, how Oscar held the tray so steadily. "I've applied for Canadian citizenship," he said.

"Uncle," Officer Ridge said, "if he's in the car with us, he's locatable. Plus which, you really should taste this cake."

"Surrender, *Arschloch*," Harnes said, and from the way he snarled it, I figured it wasn't a kind word.

"I'm a civilian," Oscar said. At which point Harnes slanted the revolver and clipped Oscar hard against his nose; blood spurted out, Oscar reeled back a few steps, but somehow managed not to drop the tray.

"Don't speak German food names in my police car," Harnes said.

I quickly opened the back door of the car and, on woozy footing, Oscar handed me the tray. He half collapsed into the car opposite me in the backseat. He shut the door behind him. He took a cloth napkin from the tray and pressed it against his nose to staunch the flow of blood, which worked. Harnes crouched into the passenger side again. I distributed the schnitzel, potato croquettes, and onion cake. Oscar closed his eyes and went silent.

Finally, he said, "I can sing 'O Canada' in French as the anthem was originally written by Mr. Calixa Lavallée."

"Spare us," Harnes said. "Will you listen to this Bavarian? Giving us locals a history lesson."

"Oscar, you might be able to outcook that famous chef Pierre Roland, down at the harbor," Officer Ridge said. "Uncle, you and me didn't have dinner last night, remember? This is delicious."

In a near whisper Oscar said, "I hope you choke on it," then looked at me and said, "Do you want me to translate that?" I shook my head no.

As he ate, Harnes said, "Look at this odd fellow. I mean, who wears a Sunday suit to cook alone in?" But Harnes kept eating.

I can't really be certain, but I think all four of us slept for a while. Just dozed off in our individual exhaustions. This is unpredictable life, I thought. Unpredictable life. As it got light out, Harnes adjusted the rearview mirror and said, "Our Bavarian looks a little worse for wear. Nephew, drop Havenshaw off at home and take our Bavarian over to NSH. Flash your badge and get him looked at. Just say Oscar here tripped facedown while walking his schnauzer."

～

WHEN I GOT BACK TO OUR HOUSE, I discovered Amelia asleep in her clothes on top of the bedclothes. She had left a note: *Exhausted. Six-hour surgery. Must take a rain check on breakfast, darling. There's eggs and bacon in the larder.* I was wide awake. I made breakfast, coffee, and at nine thirty walked to the *Evening Mail.* There was the usual distracted bustle and clacking of typewriters. I saw that Albanie Musgrave was in her office. I knocked on her door and went right in without being asked.

"Toby," she said, "know what the secret to a good night's sleep is? A spouse who's still got a pulse in the bedroom. Then a twenty-six-year-old single malt whiskey."

"I'm happy for you."

"From the look on your face, you want right away to get into deep water with me."

"Petit-de-Grat?"

"I'm your editor. That's your assignment. In between now

and when you leave for Petit-de-Grat, your beat is the court-rooms. Your old familiar haunt. Welcome back."

"I don't feel welcome."

"As for Petit-de-Grat, Spanish flu is covered by every other newspaper in the world. Why shouldn't we make more of an effort to cover it. You're the effort."

Albanie put on her reading glasses, picked up her editing pencil, and crossed out a line of copy. Without looking up, she said, "Give my best to Amelia."

As I was leaving the newsroom, the editor of the shipping news, Martin Strobe, said, "Toby, you got another call from Magistrate Spencer."

"What'd he say?"

"His Highness has summoned you. It's raining out, by the way."

Indeed, it had begun to rain hard. By the time I reached the courthouse, I was soaked through. Presentable or not, I was ushered into Magistrate Spencer's office.

"Care for a towel from my private bathroom?" he said.

"No thanks. I'll stand. You've got that nice leather chair, I wouldn't want it to rust."

"I don't have much time for chitchat. So let me tell you straightaway: Elizabeth Frame and Peter Lear were taken in for two full weeks at the Trappist Monastery at St. George's Bay, up in Antigonish County. That's about two hundred fifty kilometers from Halifax. They were fed and clothed. According to the Trappist monks, Elizabeth worried she might lose her child, travels were so arduous. She thought she might be running a fever, but as it turned out she wasn't. Anyway, our fugitives were fed and clothed and the recipients of every possible hospitality.

When asked by our operatives, the monks had no idea where they were heading next, and said operatives felt the monks were to be believed."

"St. George's Bay makes for quite the roundabout to Halifax."

"I stand firm in my conviction. She's carrying Oscar Asch's child, so come hell or high water, Oscar Asch is her destination. What Peter Lear's design is, I can't imagine."

"Thanks for keeping me apprised."

⁓

THIS EVENING, Amelia and I finally had a meal together.

"I had Bavarian food for the first time," I said. I explained as best I could the incident in front of 118 Kane.

"My gracious me, you encountered Elizabeth's first husband, then," Amelia said.

"Yes, it was Oscar Asch, all right."

"I clearly remember us at a pub with Sergeant Harnes. I can't quite recall his wife's name, but I can recall that she was long-suffering."

"Harnes's police-officer nephew's long-suffering with him, too."

"Do you like this codfish stew?"

"Delicious. Perfect."

"I got the recipe from the sister of the woman I operated on. My patient's recovering nicely. The nurses brought her some magazines. Little acts of kindness, you see."

"Would you say you had quite a night?"

"Yes, quite a night. And you, my love. Would you say the same?"

"Quite a night, yes. A night spent with police."

After a brandy it went unspoken that we would sit in the bathtub together. How something unspoken actually occurs is, to me at least, one of the loveliest mysteries of marriage. Amelia went up and ran a bath and slipped into the tub. I got in with her. Facing the same direction, she leaned back against me. Everything from there remained unspoken. Certain things should never be measured in terms of time, so let's just say that in a while we toweled off and got into bed.

Amelia said, "I never told you this, but my aunt Iona gave me sex advice, one night when she was very drunk. I was, oh, maybe fourteen. I wanted to hear everything she knew and did. And Auntie was obliging."

"What kind of advice, exactly?"

"Well, Auntie had a way, especially when inebriated, of using language that seemed to be from an earlier time. You know, back when people implied more than they said. For instance, I remember her saying, 'It's best after consummation to try and maintain an atmosphere.'"

I thought about that a moment. "Should we get back into the bathtub?"

"No, we can maintain an atmosphere right here."

CALL IT DIVINE INTERVENTION

Journal entry August 19, 1918. 3:20 a.m. Halifax

"The Second Transcript"
"An Unconfirmed Report"

SOMETIMES WEEKS UPON WEEKS PASS WITHOUT writing in this journal. But I want to now record that a second transcript addressed to me arrived to the *Evening Mail*. I copy it out here. Reading, it struck me as Elizabeth's true confession.

Remember, I already had a wedding night. With Oscar. With Oscar, during our consummation, I kept my eyes open, and then fell asleep later, so did Oscar. I had never before slept side by side with someone. It was strange and wonderful and I slept well. But with Everett, on my second wedding night, it was the opposite. During which consummation I'd kept my eyes closed. Then Everett fell asleep. But I went to the window.

Just before the wedding in St. George's Church, I had tucked a letter—in its envelope—I had tucked a letter from Oscar in a private place beneath my wedding dress. I felt it there during the vows. What kind of woman does such a thing? A woman such as me, who is me and only me, I suppose. And during the wedding and the reception, I kept thinking to myself, Who is getting married here? I stood outside of myself. When Rector Shrevard bestowed his blessing, do you know what I thought? I thought, Rector Shrevard had kicked Mrs. Buttermore's goat. I was only ten when I saw him do that. The goat had wandered behind the church. Rector Shrevard, who had preached kindness to all living things, had kicked the goat. There was no rea-

son to have done. *None that I could see at least. And the goat never quite walked right after that. So at the very moment Rector Shrevard was about to ask, "Do you, Elizabeth, take..." I actually whispered quite loudly to him, "I saw what you did to Mrs. Buttermore's goat." Nobody else but Everett could hear it. At first Rector Shrevard looked like he had no idea what I was talking about. Then it dawned on him. He then continued on, "Do you, Elizabeth, take Everett Milford Dewis to be your lawful wedded husband?"*

There's only a yes or no answer at that moment, isn't there? Don't you think that's not right? There's so many ideas, concerns, opinions in between yes and no at such a moment, isn't there, for a woman, don't you think? I suppose I could have said, "Well, except that I'm already married..." Had I done that, all hell would have broken loose, but there would have been no need to send those three morsels into Everett. But in the moment, Oscar seemed a world away.

Everyone left the church and walked to the tables. There was the prayer said and there was food and a wedding cake made by Cynthia Hawthorne, who'd so expertly secured it in her wagon, and traveled down from Joggins. Not a crumb out of place, either. Me and Everett had the first dance. And I suppose somewhat to his credit, while we danced, he said, "Now I know what happened to Mrs. Buttermore's goat." Well, I said, my timing might've been better but I did tell the truth. The dance seemed for an eternity.

In our candlelit room in Ottawa House, Everett was good with sweet nothings but his hands fell short of expertise. And of course I was committing adultery and my goodness someone of lesser discipline might've fainted dead away from the secret of it all, I suppose. After consummation, naturally, I was afraid that Everett might comment on the one obvious thing, but he didn't. Which brings me to why did Everett even have his military revolver in his satchel in the first place? I had seen it when he'd opened his satchel to take out a nightshirt. My my my, listen to me, the mind jumps around, doesn't it, just goes wherever it goddamn pleases, doesn't it?

In the bed, he'd asked me if I was a spiritual person. I replied, "I was, then I wasn't, and now I am again, but not quite with the same conviction." He said that the war made spiritual men and women out of many who previously had not been spiritual—but also vice versa. He said that he was now permanently one of the vice versa. Though if I wanted him to be spiritual with our children, he'd be fine with that. "I'll walk you to and from church," he said. Then he fell asleep.

And I've come to think of what happened next as divine intervention.

I was dressed only in my body, and I felt like an unclad spirit being beckoned. I saw the whale. I saw it right away. How could something so enormous not have woken everyone in the village just from its enormity? But it had been delivered silently to us. I imagined it to be still breathing. I studied it from the window, I thought it might still be breathing. But probably it wasn't. I know that now.

No human heart is big enough to accommodate a whale set down by the Bay of Fundy like that. I don't care what anyone says. Not even Francis of Assisi's heart would've been big enough.

Deep sorrow, the whale. The guilt, the infidelity, the desire to be elsewhere, the moonlight helping me see the whale so much in detail. What components lifted me up and drew me to the window, and those same components made for my fall from grace. "Darling, come to the window. A whale has intervened on our wedding night."

Anyway, no question, Everett was awake enough to have heard me. Because he said, "It will be there in the morning."

What happened next was a deliberate act, but a deliberate act as if in a dream. But definitely in what happened next, I was calculating. I went into the satchel, took out the revolver. "Everett, here comes a dry morsel." Rector Shrevard would be proud of me; you just never know when a passage from the Bible will come in handy. You just never know.

I was unclad. Everett's nightshirt was on the chair. I slipped it on and went downstairs. By the time I reached the whale, the revolver felt so heavy, I could scarcely hold it. Why did Everett keep it loaded, I have no idea. Some men need a revolver close by. I suddenly noticed I carried the revolver right-handed, and here I am left-handed. I hardly remember what had come before or what came after. But from the instant I was immediately with the whale, I recall everything. A whale is a planet in the water, Robert Louis Stevenson said. And so I lay my head against the planet and felt peace in my heart. You lean against a whale, your only dignity is in the recognition of your smallness. What I said to the whale was, "I am sorry this happened to you. Though I know that everything must die." I have no shame in this.

My thoughts were entirely with the whale. In that moment I felt nothing for Everett. So that is what I became that night. And that is what I am.

The transcript ends here.

WHEN THE NEXT MORNING AT 11 A.M. I brought the
transcript to Magistrate Spencer's office, he right away informed
me, "Elizabeth Frame and Peter Lear spent two nights in a
lying-in hospital in County Harbo, just south of Monastery. They
walked in and Elizabeth claimed complications with her preg-
nancy. They were taken in right away, no questions asked. Our
information has it that there were no medical complications."

"Elizabeth is with child and on the lam. That's complications enough."

"I suppose that's true."

I held up the envelope in clear view. "Maybe this new transcript was sent from County Harbo. Or Monastery earlier."

"Or maybe Petit-de-Grat."

"Petit-de-Grat?"

"We have an unconfirmed report that they might've gone to
Petit-de-Grat. But there's rampant influenza in that region. My
operatives are begging off the place."

"I can't help but imagine that Albanie Musgrave told you she
assigned me to Petit-de-Grat."

"Human interest story, she said."

I handed him the envelope. He sat down and read the transcript straight through, now and then shaking his head back and
forth, or muttering, "Unusual mind." I sat there looking out the
window onto the street.

When he was done reading, he said, "She's as close to Dante
as Parrsboro's ever going to produce," seemingly without irony.
"You have a copy, I presume." I nodded yes. "All that zigzag
spouting off. Could she be shrewdly providing evidence of her

being unfit to stand trial? Interpretation of that statute would be at the pleasure of the lieutenant governor."

"I'm pretty sure she doesn't have any law books with her," I said, "to look such things up in."

"Why is she sending the transcripts to you, I wonder."

"I think it's because I had a connection with Peter Lear. I think Lear told her of our connection. I think he told Elizabeth that he spoke of personal things with a crime reporter from the *Evening Mail*. I think Elizabeth wants her story to be told."

I left Magistrate Spencer's office.

⌒

DURING OUR PILLOW TALK THAT NIGHT, I said to Amelia, "I now have a clear plan."

"Does it have to do with leaving the *Evening Mail*? Because I hope it does."

"In fact, yes. But first I'm going to write a very good piece about Petit-de-Grat."

"And then you'll tell Albanie Musgrave she's a hag and you never liked her and you never liked working for her."

"Good words to fall back on."

"My opinion aside, what do you imagine comes next?"

"I'm not sure. Except that I'll continue to write privately about Elizabeth and Peter, and when I'm eventually done, I'll march right on over to Homer and hand it to him. 'Homer, you can have this if you want it.'"

"I have every confidence you'll be hired on the spot. He's been wanting to hire you on the spot."

Amelia took me through her day, gossip from nurses, the fact that she "needs a holiday." We shared a long silence, and then Amelia said, "I say good riddance to Albanie Musgrave. And that puts a lid on that pot, right?" I knew this about my wife, she did not leave a subject until she wanted to leave it.

"Right as rain."

THERE ARE THIRTY EVIL DAYS COMING

Journal entry October 7, 1918. 5:20 a.m. Halifax

"Amelia's Instructions"

LIFE HAS BEEN FULL, LIFE HAS BEEN BUSY. I'VE been covering the courtrooms, which has been full of a numbing redundancy. But I continue to earn my paycheck. I have had three updates on Elizabeth and Peter from Magistrate Spencer, but all three have mostly been speculation. Plus which, I've had little inclination to write in this journal until now.

Yesterday in the *Evening Mail*, there was an article whose headline was "The Influenza Epidemic Has Not Reached Halifax and We Are Fighting Its Advances":

Citizens Are Readily Complying With Orders From the Health Board—Churches, Schools and Theatres Are Closed

HALIFAX, OCTOBER 6

The Spanish influenza situation in Halifax is encouraging. The epidemic stage has not yet been reached. The precautionary measures taken by the board of health appear to be having effect in preventing the spread of the disease it was hoped that it would. Since Saturday official reports show that the disease has made but a very slight gain and by the end of the present week it is believed that it will be definitely known whether Halifax is to be swept by an epidemic similar to that expe-

rienced in Massachusetts and in some of the large Canadian cities. Unless the disease shows signs of developing during the week the drastic order issued by the health board, closing the churches, schools, theatres and all other public places and stopping persons from congregating may be rescinded. Since Saturday only four new cases were reported to the board of health, two of these, being military cases, were taken care of by the military authorities at the Cogswell street hospital. Only about four cases of the disease are in the new isolation hospital, controlled by the city on Morris street. The health board has decided to use this building to the fullest capacity for the treatment of patients with the disease.

The health board experienced little difficulty in enforcing the orders issued for the closing of all public places and against the overcrowding of streets and the congregating of persons. The citizens seemed to realize the seriousness of the situation, obeying the order in a creditable manner. The Tramway company is using every effort to rigidly enforce the order against the overcrowding of the cars. Signs have been posted at the entrance of all cars, calling attention to the order of the health board that there must be no overcrowding and no standing in the cars. Those in control of the cars were instructed to use their best endeavors to enforce the order.

The initial enforcement of it on Saturday morning caused some unpleasantness and interfered with the operation of the cars on schedule, but later in the day, even during the rain, the people seemed to appreciate the position of the conductors and the conductresses and cooperated with them in carrying out the new order. Very few cars were found to be carrying more passengers than there was seating accommodation for. Many persons *walked rather than take the risk of being infected with the disease by riding on the cars.*

The theatres, as a rule, complied with the order and will continue to do so until it is rescinded by the health board. All places of amusement will be closed.

Apropos of this article, last evening at dinner at our kitchen table, Amelia said she'd read it.

"Toby, influenza has in fact reached Halifax," she said, highly annoyed. "My hospital is already overwhelmed. Your paper is misleading people—it's lying. But do you know what? Professor Ellman, who teaches all sorts of mythologies and psychologies at Dalhousie—I met him in the waiting room the other day. His wife Alice has Spanish flu and she is not going to make it. She may already be gone. I sat with him a short while. He said that if you study the mythologies of dozens of different cultures, one thing that becomes clear is that the most destructive demons— the ones that wreak the most havoc, that screw up people's minds mercilessly—are the invisible ones. That's what Spanish flu is. But it's not 'on its way' to Halifax. It's arrived. It's here."

And a few days earlier, the *Evening Standard* published, with her permission, a diary entry by L. M. Montgomery that was titled "There Are Thirty Evil Days Coming." Maybe because she's married to a Baptist minister she feels she can strike a prophetic note—on the other hand, how hard can it be to predict evil days, at this point in 1918?

In following the war reports in various newspapers, you come to realize what was true yesterday at noon is not true today at noon—The British line held but Neuve-Église was lost. Then, worse: The Germans are sweeping on to the Aisne. Then they've got to Château-Thierry—an outpost of Paris. Then the French counterattacked in the Château-Thierry region. It's like checking Europe's temperature every half hour. We're all being driven mad by war and Spanish flu.

Amelia reached across the table and took my hands in hers. "About Petit-de-Grat," she said. "You can't protect me from Spanish flu when I go to hospital every day—and then I come home and kiss my husband as often as possible, so I can't protect you even from myself. And if you go up to Petit-de-Grat, who knows what you'll find there? I know I'm not supposed to tell you not to go. But is there any way you don't have to go? If Albanie wants a human interest story on Spanish flu, what about my very own hospital, right here in Halifax. You come to work with me. You go on rounds with a few doctors."

"I like that idea, but Albanie won't. Once she assigns something, it's written in stone."

"That's exactly what worries me—and I'm not being ironic. Because you know what gets written in stone."

"Petit-de-Grat's not going to be my epitaph."

"I hate the world just now. Where will you sleep?"

"St. Joseph's Church. It's all been arranged. I probably won't stay for more than two or three nights."

"And the paper will provide a touring car?"

"Yes."

"For the record, I disagree with this whole thing. But like I said, I go into hospital every day, don't I. And I kiss my husband every chance I get. Still, I'm very much against you going to Petit-de-Grat. Just for the record."

"Of course, just for the record."

"Don't eat anything local, even if a codfish jumps directly

from the sea onto your plate. Pack enough food from home that won't spoil. Bread and cheese. Cookies." She went to the counter, found a piece of paper and wrote on it, then set it in front of me. "As you know, I'm highly organized."

"The world's greatest understatement."

The piece of paper read:

DRIVE ALONE IN TOURING CAR TO PETIT-DE-GRAT

SPEAK TO PEOPLE ONLY THROUGH DOORS AND WINDOWS

DO NOT SHAKE ANYONE'S HAND

WASH YOUR HANDS WITH SOAP EVERY CHANCE YOU GET

USE THE PROTECTIVE MASKS I PROVIDE

"Dr. Morley, will these precautions work?" I said.

"I suppose they give you a fighting chance."

"Better than nothing,"

"What's that thing Heraclitus wrote? In Peter Lear's book you keep leaving around the house. Oh yes. 'To compare impossibilities can never be solacing. But at least provides a perspective.' That's not it word for word, but almost."

"I get it. I'll compare the hope of not getting deathly ill to barely escaping getting deathly ill."

"And not even knowing how close you came."

"Interesting you've looked at Peter Lear's book."

"Oh, I've read it cover to cover."

"Find any of it useful? At the hospital, I mean."

"Some days, yes. Most days, no."

Both of us tossed and turned all night. "Are you awake?"—1 a.m. "Are you awake?"—3 a.m. "Are you still awake?"—4 a.m. Then I made us breakfast.

PETIT-DE-GRAT

Journal entry October 15, 1918. 3:45 a.m. Halifax

"Fiddler's Woe"
"Death of Elizabeth Frame"
"The Child"

ALBANIE HAD PROVIDED ME WITH A PACKET OF research. The basic facts were these: Spanish flu broke out in Petit-de-Grat per se when the *Athlete* made port there. The schooner had come up from the Caribbean and arrived with a full load of salt for the Comeau Brothers fish plant. Most of the crew had already fallen ill. Local citizens of Petit-de-Grat unloaded the salt, and after that Spanish flu quickly spread through the village and neighboring parishes. A few people thought the flu was the revenge of the Germans, whose spies poisoned the wells and coughed into vials full of infected air they secretly released in stores and churches and schools. One Henry Sheeran was quoted as saying, "Black rum ingested in quantity is both preventative and curative." To which another person said, "Well, that's Henry—that's how he approaches every day of his life, whether he's sick or not." In those first days of the epidemic, fear and blame went wild. Albanie somehow obtained a list of the victims so far in association with Petit-de-Grat. One little boy, James Bouchie, who died on October 17, was just fifteen months old. "No matter how difficult," wrote Heraclitus, "your journey on this earth is paradise." I thought, Try convincing James Bouchie of that.

I had little interest in writing a human interest piece about Petit-de-Grat. Not that I didn't care about the life of that village. I did care. But heart and soul, I mainly was invested in the possibility of setting eyes on Elizabeth Frame and Peter Lear. I'd covered dozens and dozens of hearings and trials. But I had always been able to forget the victim and accused almost right away. But not this time. Amelia told me one morning that I'd said in my sleep, "It's that damn whale's fault," just that one sentence uttered in the dark. Of course, it all had something to do with telling Elizabeth and Peter's story. But really it had become a blinder passion than that. And I think it all begged a larger question. Was this all moving toward being a genuine tragedy? I think I wanted Elizabeth and Peter to define *tragedy* for me. Or was I simply incapable of recognizing it as pathetic: two people whose lives commingled like dust and rain, without rhyme or reason, or even real meaning? In the end, I knew little about them, really. And yet my heart went out to them.

"I think in some way you've come to love them both," Amelia said, quite matter-of-factly. We were having a brandy.

"I'm loath to love a murderer and a besotted fool."

"Maybe you just want to be seen as someone loath to love a murderer. But really you may be someone who in fact does. Obviously I don't mean romantic love, Toby. I mean maybe you're just mesmerized by devastating fates. It all quickens your heart somehow." I must have had a certain expression, because Amelia then said, "Don't give me that puzzled look. You know exactly what I mean."

Some days after I left at first light and traveled to Petit-de-Grat, and set up in St. Joseph's Church by seven o'clock that night. As I entered the village, the fishing port silence was broken by the crying of gulls. The sea slapping against hulls of fishing trawlers. The eeriness of houses, some painted in pastel colors, with boarded-up windows. Makeshift wooden crosses, haphazardly located, not in a cemetery. Two horses grazing on weeds behind the church. Chill salt wind off the sea. A sign in front of a house in which, as I later found out, all six members of a family died of Spanish flu: THE DEVIL EXHALED HERE. I had entered a moonlit and deeply suffering village.

The church was cold and naturally I had my choice of pews; I chose toward the front. I was grateful for the blankets and quilts I'd brought along, and I also wore a second sweater under my coat. If I thought it might have done any good, I'd have prayed for sleep. Finally, exhaustion replaced the need for prayer and I slept soundly, for the first time in months. I woke thinking first thing that I should tell Amelia that I want to sleep on a church pew from now on—just to try and make her laugh. I opened the door to cloudy daylight and the crying of gulls. I drank water from my thermos. I pissed out back the church. I ate bread and cheese. I shaved using my strop razor and combed my hair using the touring car's rearview mirror. Then I set out to try and talk to anyone who'd talk to me, through doors and windows.

I visited eight houses in all. I made a map of Petit-de-Grat in my notebook. I'd knock on a door. If someone called out, I'd say, "Toby Havenshaw, Halifax *Evening Mail*. I'm writing a human interest story. People want to know how the citizens of Petit-de-Grat are getting by. Can we talk for a few minutes?"

For Petit-de-Grat having the reputation of being a religious village, language-wise I got a number of irreligious responses, you might say. "If you call what's going on here 'getting by,' you have your head up your own ass!" Also the Lord's name taken in vain. I kind of admired the honesty of it. The Lord's name taken in vain by mouths I couldn't see. Most often I received stark and final declarations. "I became a widow and orphan in the same week." "My children were Abel, Corinne, and Charlotte. They're gone. Do you expect to be invited in for tea?" "As for the difficulty of not having my husband, you don't get to make an angel toast and jam." "My marriage to Edward was never rancorous, thirty-nine years. Do you know what it is to lose that? Have a safe journey home." I wrote these and others in my notebook; not their last words, I hoped.

At dusk on my first full day in Petit-de-Grat, as I lay on the pew and used my coat as a pillow, it fully registered to me that I'd only seen one actual person in the flesh so far. That had come about in an odd way. I'd knocked on the front door of a house overlooking the harbor. In a sidelong glance through the door's small window, I thought I saw someone. So I began to talk loudly, almost to shout, "I'm Toby Havenshaw, from the *Evening Mail!*"

I went on like that for a good two or three minutes, a kind of rant of commiseration, about the etherizing effects of Spanish flu on the human spirit. I tried to come off as spiritual, but it might've sounded complete rot. Hoping for any sort of engagement. It wasn't working.

I kept my voice raised for a little longer and finally heard from behind me a man's voice: "I know the city is loud—but does everyone shout like that? Sir—!"

I turned to see a fellow of about fifty years of age, give or take. He was carrying a can of paint. Two paintbrushes peeked up from the side pocket of his coat.

"Sir—I know you're the newspaper reporter staying in our church," he said. "And I know you're trying your best. But you should know, the Donovan family who lived in the house whose door you just knocked on, they left Petit-de-Grat three weeks ago to the day. Nobody's inside. I thought that'd be useful information. Now, I'm going down to repaint the cabin of my boat. I'm thinking of living on my trawler for a while. Good sea air circulating in my lungs and I can fish from deck. I've even got a small woodstove there. I put that in specially."

He walked down to the dock. I wrote down what he'd said. Maybe not perfectly stenographic, but close to it.

Next morning I woke early and went through the ritual of having a bite to eat, cleaning up my person, getting my notebooks in order. Then I walked to a house situated on a rise. From fifty or sixty meters away, a little encouragement: smoke billowed from the chimney. When I reached the house, I knocked on the front door, but there was no response. But in another minute or two, there came an insistent hollow knocking originating to my left. I stepped from the porch and went to the window, which was not boarded up. I peered inside.

There stood Peter Lear.

He had an untrimmed beard and looked severely worse for wear. But I recognized him right away. He wore the same clothes he'd had on the second day of the hearing, all those months before. I'd been so hopeful of encountering Elizabeth and Peter in Petit-de-Grat, I'd tucked the Heraclitus book into my satchel. So right away I took it out and pressed it to the window. Peter looked exhilarated, even tearful. However, his degraded countenance went unchanged. He stepped back from the window and walked a few steps to a table on which he'd placed the stenographic machine. He sat in a chair and tapped out some words, tore them from the scroll, walked back and placed the paper against the glass. It read: *I believe Elizabeth is dying. Life in ruins. Come back this afternoon. Bedroom in back. This is the doctor's house*. I nodded that I understood, and then I left the premises, fairly reeling from what had just occurred.

I've often found that when I feel particularly useless, a little physical work helps. I walked down to the dock and hallooed to the fellow I'd spoken with earlier. He was busy painting the outside of his trawler's cabin. On the hull was the name *Fiddler's Woe*. I thought, What a name, as if the trawler itself could, with the help of whistling sea winds, play a dirge, and where better for a dirge these days than Petit-de-Grat.

He set down the brush and walked to the rail. "I'm Windsor Tennyson," he said. "From Dartmouth originally, but I've lived in Petit-de-Grat thirty years now."

"Toby Havenshaw."

"I heard you introduce yourself to an empty house, remember?"

"Right."

"Climb aboard. I've got butter scones and coffee."

"I don't want to get too close."

"I don't want you too close. Now that's a quick gentlemen's agreement, isn't it."

On deck, I said, "I wonder if I might help you paint."

"You come to Petit-de-Grat. You're met by what you're met by. You need to pass the time. I understand that. Yours is a friendly offer. I accept. Those nice clothes might get splattered. That can't be helped. But let's keep a good distance apart so we don't kill each other. My Lord, did I just say that? This plague has made me forget my own humanity. Coffee and scones are on the bench there."

There was little breeze to speak of. Our voices carried well enough through the open door. He worked on the interior, I worked on the exterior; I could hear his brushstrokes, which sounded a little like sandpaper. Gulls on the rail just would not shut up.

"I'd take a potshot if you could eat that bird," Tennyson said. "Did you get anyone to talk to you yet?"

"Not a soul."

"They've most of them gone inward. Me myself too to some extent, I've gone inward. Then again, I've lost my two closest friends, and a boy who scraped and cleaned fish for me for nearly two years died in his sleep, and all the mercy for that. Also, he could whistle Beethoven. He'd only have to hear it once on the phonograph and could whistle it."

"Not a whole symphony, of course."

"No, but long passages."

We didn't talk for a while, until Tennyson said, "The house you were just at. The one painted yellow. I saw you staring into the window. Those two come-from-aways—well, three, really, as the woman is with child. They arrived to Petit-de-Grat, I'd say about three weeks ago, though the calendar's a gone pigeon of late—I mean, what with so many deaths, daily life seems replaced by eternity—it's a goddamned unusual sensation for the average person like me. Anyway, an automobile left them in front of the church, then drove off. The roads may be poorly kept but they'd made it. One satchel and one leather suitcase between them. The fellow has a contraption of some sort."

"It's a stenographic machine. He's a court stenographer. Or was. You type out what's said in courtroom proceedings."

"I've heard of that. I don't know why they ended up here, for God's sake. That might be a mystery impossible to solve, but what does it matter, they were here, and despite the fact that myself among others cited all the local deaths from Spanish flu and begged them to leave, they stayed. You can't turn away exhausted people in trouble, now can you."

"Their names are—" I said, but Tennyson interrupted, "I know their names. Elizabeth and Peter. We don't live on the moon. We get a newspaper. Believe it or not, long before they showed up in Petit-de-Grat, those two were included in a church sermon, only a Sunday before the church closed down. It was a Christian inquiry-type sermon: how do we judge, or how shouldn't we judge, lost souls. Well, when this Elizabeth and Peter arrived straight out of the newspaper and assorted word of mouth, I thought to myself, Their souls are definitely lost if they end up in Petit-de-Grat under present conditions."

"Peter informed me it was the doctor's house."

"That would be our local physician, Richard O'Shee, and his wife Catherine. And this Elizabeth and Peter were out front with Dr. and Mrs. O'Shee from the get-go. They didn't lie. They said the law was not pleased with them."

"Quaintly put. Elizabeth murdered her husband in Parrsboro."

"Like I said, they were out front."

"The sheer fact of it didn't bother you?"

"Bothers me a lot. But a person sizes up each situation as it comes, and you're either charitable toward it or you aren't charitable. Richard and Catherine O'Shee chose to be charitable. They didn't ask for a vote on the matter."

"Have the O'Shees been sick?"

"So far, no."

"Peter told me that Elizabeth might be at death's door."

"Oh, I am truly sorry to hear that, as she's with child, that is very sad news. But also because she's in such close quarters with Richard and Catherine."

"I hope theirs is a good deed that goes unpunished."

"Let's wait and see."

I noticed here and there that I'd applied paint carelessly, so touched things up in those places. We worked for a couple of hours. And actually we spoke very little, past the initial conversation.

Finally, Tennyson said, "In my house, I have an electric blanket. Have you ever seen one of those? I think it might be a fairly recent invention. I hadn't known of it till my niece sent me one from Halifax. I'd loan it to you but there's no electric socket in the church."

"I'm fine, thanks. I appreciate having a place to sleep."

"I won't shake your hand. But it was nice meeting you. Thanks for helping out."

"You did me a favor."

"Good luck to you, then. I've got things to do now."

I walked back to the church and slept a while and had a dream of the whale. I won't go into details, but I will say that I wished I hadn't dreamed it. It made me feel the accidental qualities of life had rudely pushed all else aside. I shook it off best I could and walked back down to the wharf. It had become a cloudless late afternoon. You could anticipate a starry night. Somehow it allowed a moment's exhilaration, just in and of itself, without purpose, really. Like taking a deep breath before facing something. I wondered if Amelia took such deep breaths just before entering the surgical theater. It was a random thought, but just then served to keep me connected to my wife.

Approaching the O'Shees' house, I again saw chimney smoke. In a few moments, as I stood back from the house about ten meters, Peter appeared in the dining room window again. Good Lord, how was it possible that he looked even more woebegone and haggard than just a few hours before? Life was a ravaging wind. He might have seen me approaching; you could see the church from the window. Peter had a message prepared and laid it flat against the window: *The child is coming.* He gestured toward the back of the house and I immediately went there.

I made a makeshift calculation, based on knowledge from the hearing in Ottawa House. Having gone to buy a wedding dress and rendezvous with Oscar Asch around March 8 or 9, and having stayed in Halifax for four days, that's when Elizabeth married and became pregnant by Oscar Asch. That would make her into her eighth month. Which meant that the child was arriving early. But Amelia had often brought home stories of premature births, as she referred to them. She said she sometimes felt that the child itself, if the mother was weak from illness, mustered up an astonishing hurry to be born, to escape the mother's failing body. "The will to live," she said. "It's the will to live." But there in Petit-de-Grat, all I really understood was the fact that, for all intents and purposes, Dr. O'Shee had decided to bring this child into the world before the date of natural childbirth. This Amelia told me was called a cesarean section, which was designed, under the best results, to spare the life of both mother and child. There might be any number of reasons, but most obvious was that if Elizabeth suddenly perished from Spanish flu, so would her child.

I didn't yet know if anyone but Peter Lear was aware of my presence. I had hoped not. I had hoped that right up to the moment that Elizabeth, pale as paper, lying in the four-poster bed, bedclothes pulled up to her neck, stared right at me and held up a book. I could read the title: *Island Nights' Entertainments* by Robert Louis Stevenson.

For some reason the things that happened next seemed to move in a kind of slow motion, but that might speak to how choreographically deliberate each person's movements were. The small bedroom had a writing desk, which was set near the woodstove. On the stove was a cauldron. Dr. O'Shee had set out operating scissors, sponges, large forceps, suturing thread and needles, washcloths. There were other items I couldn't quite make out. Peter stood left of the bed and close to the wall. Dr. O'Shee was administering an anesthetic, I imagine chloroform, by pressing a soaked cloth to Elizabeth's face. Soon I saw that Elizabeth had gone under. Dr. O'Shee listened to her heart with his stethoscope. I noticed that *Island Nights' Entertainments* lay at Peter's feet. Dr. O'Shee gestured and spoke to Peter, who promptly added a log to the fire. Dr. O'Shee lifted two surgical gloves from the cauldron with a spatula, set the spatula and gloves on a cloth on the table, waited a moment before he put on the gloves. Mrs. O'Shee then sat next to Elizabeth on the bed, lowered the bedclothes to below Elizabeth's feet. I could see a folded set of sheets on a shelf in the open armoire. Peter changed locale in the room, so that now Elizabeth's body was mostly hidden from my view. Also, the window was a little steamed over. I suppose I was grateful for this. Maybe I had no right to see any of it; I almost resented Peter inviting me to. I think he must've felt incredibly alone in all of this. In less than half an hour by my estimation, Peter's hand holding a cloth wiped in arcs across the window. The first thing I noticed was that the bedclothes had been drawn up over Elizabeth's face. And following that I noticed Mrs. O'Shee holding the swaddled child. Peter gestured for me to go to the front of the house, which I promptly did. I stayed well back from the front door. When Peter opened it, he said, "Kindly leave my Heraclitus on the porch here."

"It was Josephine Huntley in Parrsboro who gave me your book in the first place," I said. "She thought we might somehow meet up."

"And here we both are. I know you saw the bedclothes drawn up."

"I did see that."

"If you turn around, you'll see a coffin on its way. Driven here by Albert Ponsot, undertaker. On the seat with him's the grave-digger Waddy Bond."

I turned and saw a horse-and-buggy hearse, with an unvarnished wood coffin in back. Ponsot was dressed in a black greatcoat, black trousers, and boots. Even with daily life so off-kilter, he maintained a professional decorum, I thought.

"How could Ponsot possibly have known when to arrive here?" I said.

"Think about it for a minute, you might conclude that's a stupid question. Still, I'll help you understand. About six this morning, Dr. O'Shee gathered me and Mrs. O'Shee into the kitchen. He told us Elizabeth's influenza had progressed to where any minute she could drown in her own lungs, is how he put it. 'Therefore I'm going declare a definite time. We might not be able to wait that long. But I'm declaring four thirty this afternoon. We'll get everything ready.' He asked me to go speak with the undertaker Ponsot. Tell him the declared time. 'Elizabeth cannot possibly survive the surgery. But God willing, her child can.'"

Some activity in the house drew Peter's attention. "I need to help out," he said.

"I won't ask what Elizabeth meant to you."

"I'll reserve that question for myself. It might take years to answer."

"I'm leaving my card tucked into your book." I handed him the Heraclitus. "Not that you'd want. Not that I could. But if there's anything I can do. By the way, I've befriended Magistrate Spencer. Though 'befriend' might be overstating it."

"Did the transcripts ever reach you?"

"Both did."

"Use them as you will. Elizabeth had even more in mind. She'd wanted to dictate from way back into her childhood but never got to. She wanted to be written about. She saw herself written about. I never judged that."

"You have my card."

"Want to know something? Elizabeth was on the same page of that Robert Louis Stevenson for about two weeks."

He went back into the house and left the door slightly open. The undertaker's horse-and-buggy had stopped out front of the house. I walked to within about ten meters.

"Newspaper, correct?" Ponsot said. "Well, you can't quote me because I'm not saying a word."

"Fair enough."

I went back to the church. I can't remember all of how the time passed. At about nine o'clock, I was sitting on a back pew. I had an oil lantern and was writing in my journal, pretty much at loose ends as to what I might write about Petit-de-Grat. Dr. O'Shee opened the door, walked in, and sat down across the aisle.

"I think we're enough distance apart here," he said. "Peter

Lear told me the father is a fellow named Oscar Asch. He needs
to be informed. It's only right. I'm directly asking you to inform
him. The child is a girl. She's healthy. Needs to put on a little
weight, but Mrs. O'Shee will see to that. My wife has the knowledge and wherewithal in such situations. I cannot really predict,
but my guess is that the child can travel within a month, five
weeks to play it safe. Unless there's something unforeseen. Peter
Lear is of little practical use. Still, he's here. He's shown no symptoms so far. I haven't asked him what he feels his responsibilities
are toward the child. He may feel he doesn't have any. My wife
and I, we'd like him to leave as soon as possible. But we won't
cast him out, either. Not just yet."

"Where's Elizabeth buried?"

"About thirty meters south of this church. She's now a neighbor with a Church of England, five Catholics, one atheist. The
latter is my own sister. Albert Ponsot painted *Elizabeth Frame*
on a wooden cross. Of course, he hadn't the slightest notion
of her denomination. We can carry lanterns there right now if
you want."

And so I walked with Dr. O'Shee to Elizabeth's grave. We
stayed only a short while. Looking up at the sky, I suddenly
remembered my mother saying, "The stars know just the right
distance to keep from each other." Given the vigilant distances
human beings have to keep from each other these days, it seemed
a magnanimous gesture that Dr. O'Shee placed his hand on
my shoulder and kept it there for a full sentence: "We took this
woman in." He lifted his hand away. "It may have been reckless
of us. But take her in we did. Looking at this sorry grave, I could
search the whole night and not locate any true feelings toward her.
But my own father used to say, 'If you can't grieve for a person

individually'—say, Elizabeth here—'you can say a prayer for their loved ones.' Elizabeth's mother, for instance, over in Parrsboro. You should notify her mother. As a newspaperman, I'm sure you have resources to do that."

"Did your father live here in Petit-de-Grat?"

"Born and raised. I took over his practice sixteen years ago. My father was well liked. I'm often well liked."

I walked with Dr. O'Shee back to the church. "Come see the child, why don't you?" he said. "I'll hold her up in front of the window, or Mrs. O'Shee will."

He then set out for home. I watched his lantern light diminish, then disappear where the road veered toward the dock. Farther on, I could see lights fore and aft on *Fiddler's Woe*, pitch dark in between. Back inside the church, incipient in mind and body, a sleepless night ahead. Such harbingers, generally cranked-up nerves and the powerful need to think too many things through, were already at work. One kind of consciousness had used up its mandate; another had replaced it. How to think about Petit-de-Grat? I had three sharpened pencils, plenty of kerosene in the lamp, dozens of empty notebook pages.

And indeed it was a sleepless night. In this regard, I suppose a cold church is not to be recommended. When I woke on the pew, I debated seeing the child but decided against. I left in the touring car just at first light. It wasn't until about 8:30 p.m. that I arrived home. Amelia was sitting at the kitchen table reading *The Return of the Soldier* by Rebecca West, which had just recently arrived to bookstores, and which Amelia told me had some fanfare.

She looked over at me in the doorway. "I'm so happy to see you, darling," she said. "Any symptoms? Sniffles. Fever. Achiness."

"That's a modern greeting."

"You married a doctor."

"Should I quarantine?"

"Did you follow my instructions to the letter?"

"Yes."

"Have a hot bath. You tell me about Petit-de-Grat. I'm not going to tell you about the hospital. I've been trying to forget everything by reading this excellent novel."

I set down my travel bag.

"Toby, was Elizabeth Frame in Petit-de-Grat?"

"Yes. And what's more, she's now buried there."

"Just tell me."

I took a quick bath and Amelia set out a bowl of potato leek soup for each of us. "Start at the beginning," she said.

And so I did. I tried not to leave anything out, but that's always a recipe for failure, isn't it. I don't know how long we talked.

"Coffee?" I said.

Once coffee was prepared and we each sat with our mug at the table again, Amelia said, "I should tell you, almost every day for the next month I've got corrective surgeries."

"Not sure what that refers to."

"Nobody really talks about it. But over in France and Belgium, field surgeries were often done on the quick. The main purpose was to save a life. The doctors called it 'repair work.' I know that's awful but we called it that. I'm speaking here of hundreds. We got bullets or shrapnel out. We patched a fellow up. Morphine. Wretched conditions. Trying to keep your eyes open. You know most of this already, Toby. I've told you everything. But every surgeon knew, every day and night, that some of these men—a lot of them, actually—would need more surgery when they got home. There's a wait list a mile long. Two miles."

"And it falls on you to perform these?" We were holding hands across the table.

"We divvy them out. I'm senior so I get to pick and choose a little. But the work is shared and shared alike. With some men it helps, but not a lot. With some it helps a lot. There's also fatalities, which is the cruelest irony of all. Just imagine, a fellow goes through what he goes through in the trenches. He gets surgery in a field hospital. He finally is shipped home. He sees his wife and children, family, whomever. He goes back into hospital and dies there. I've seen this up close. Every one of us has. Nobody really talks about it."

"You look exhausted. I hope you sleep well."

"I'll be practically living in hospital. Why not set up right here at home, right at this table, and write the human interest story for Albanie, I mean. Then save Elizabeth for Homer at the *Standard*. Get your paycheck from the *Mail* and kiss Albanie Musgrave good-bye."

"What if I transfer Spanish flu to her that way?"

"If you ever really actually kissed her, I'd have your mail forwarded to the indigents' hotel on Gottingen Street."

We were trying to find just the right tone and sweetness to bridge the days we'd had to sleep apart.

"You don't hide love letters from me, do you?" she said. "I've heard murder attracts a certain type."

"I got one recently"—which was true—"it said something along the lines of, 'You write well on your chosen subject. But what kind of person does that make you?'"

"That's not fair. As if fairness can be expected."

"Food for thought, though, don't you think? In the midnight hour, food for thought."

Amelia set the glass salt shaker in front of her. She wrapped a cloth napkin around her forehead and rubbed the salt shaker, then stared into it. In a thick accent of unknown origin, she read my fortune. "I see a surgery to remove murder from your future. Someone other than your wife performs it, in order to avoid recriminations. I see a miraculous recovery, just a day or two. I see notebooks. I see a typewriter. I see a 'Do Not Disturb' sign from a hotel room, but hung so it's flat against your back. I see a stack of paper. I see a title page. I see the title."

"Which is what?"

Amelia brought the salt shaker close to her face, stared into it, and said, "Ah, that will cost extra."

"But we haven't discussed a fee at all."

"I'll exact the price in bed soon."

"But what's the title?"

"*How to Pray for Sleep.*" She'd stopped using her fortune-teller's voice.

"Say, that's not too bad. A little sentimental, though."

"Worried about gaining too large an audience? It's not like saying a prayer is practical advice."

"I'll think it over."

"I've just noticed you've got a little soap in your ear."

"Hours now, we've talked about what we've talked about. And that's what you have to say? I've got soap in my ear."

"I've always had a personal touch in conversation. Call it my bedside manner. It's one of the reasons you love me."

Amelia's face all but collapsed in thought, a definite turn in mood. But I could see she couldn't help it. Something had happened. She took off the cloth napkin and set it on the table. She placed the salt shaker next to the pepper shaker. She closed her eyes, sighed deeply, and said, "My supervisor called me into her office. She said there'd been a report."

"Report?"

"That I've become persnickety with my staff. That my general comportment has become . . . chilly. I just didn't recognize myself in this."

"You've been under tremendous pressure. Plus you're sleeping poorly."

"It gets worse. Well, maybe not worse, exactly. Stranger."

"Just tell me."

"Apparently last week. When doing the regular prep. You know, I go through each procedure with the anesthesiologist, the nurses, everyone. This particular patient's name was Edward Chalfrin. He needed residual shrapnel removed from the abdomen. Apparently, when I spoke of his originally having had surgery at Arques, I got noticeably worked up—noticeably even to me. Of course, it was nearly midnight and I'd had three surgeries that day already. Edward Chalfrin had been brought in through emergency. The shrapnel had moved. It had resituated itself. This happens more than you'd think. But while reciting the patient's history, I referred to him as 'Creighton McBurnie,' and realizing I'd done that, I just broke down in tears. But not in front of everyone—I'd gone to my office first, thank God."

"The fellow you had nightmares about—Creighton McBurnie. That time or two I had to wake you up, that's the fellow, right?"

"I even wondered if it was me who originally operated on Edward Chalfrin in Arques. It's possible, you know."

"What did your supervisor suggest?"

"Oh, he's seen everything, Dr. Sheehan has. With all of us, he's seen everything. But he did put the hammer down. So it's to be only one corrective surgery per day, through the month of corrective surgeries. Then I'm to take two weeks' rest and recuperation. I was thinking of my colleague's family home— Bethany Bates—in Advocate Harbor. You remember our weekend there, what was it, four years ago? Everything's perfect for it. All I'd have to do is unpack my novels. Eat. Sleep. Walk along the beach looking for driftwood."

"Can I visit you there?"

"I'd have to limit your visit to fourteen days and nights out of the two weeks."

"It's a wonderful house."

"By the way, from my supervisor it wasn't a suggestion. It was marching orders. I'm to take two weeks away. To be followed by an evaluation. He said the evaluation's pro forma. Presumably everything then returns to normal. Believe me, I'm hardly the first. In the past two years, at least half the surgical staff residents have been thus instructed. It's for everyone's benefit. Staff. Patients. Everyone."

"Good. This will be a good thing."

⌒

WHEN I WOKE, Amelia was not there. She had left a note: *Sleepyhead, you didn't even hear the door at 4 a.m.! I got called in for an emergency. I'm anyway all day at hospital. Maybe you'll go to Haliburton for dinner—sorry, my darling.*

I worked at the public library much of the day, both on the

piece about Petit-de-Grat as well as doing research on insomnia in three different sections: psychology, history, medical. The former felt public, the latter private—that was my way of separating the two writing projects. I took Amelia's advice and had dinner at Haliburton House Inn: roast chicken, rice, acorn squash, plus a glass of wine. Sitting there at the corner table, I decided I'd go see Oscar Asch first thing in the morning. I knew I should have already done so. I jotted down a few ideas of what to say to him and how to say it.

When I got home around 8:30 p.m., I was surprised to find an envelope taped to the front door. I tore it open. *Toby, come immediately to the hospital. Ask for me at the nurses' station. Immediately please.* This can't be good, I thought. That Amelia had sent someone to the house like that. Was she herself all right? She's at risk of Spanish flu every day. You can't help where your mind goes. I hurried to the hospital.

At the nurses' station I asked for Dr. Morley. Two of the nurses recognized me. I was given a surgical mask and brought immediately to Recovery Room 115. Amelia was standing next to the bed. There was a nurse and another doctor there as well. All wore surgical masks. When she saw me, Amelia walked over and embraced me and said, "The world's just too much just now."

Then she stepped back and said, "Toby, this is Mary Origo and Dr. Sabine. Dr. Sabine assisted me in surgery." Both Mary Origo and Dr. Sabine left the room. The patient was hooked up to a saline drip. His face was bruised and disfigured, his head bandaged like a mummy. There was a line of stitches under his left eye. But I knew it was worse than what I could see. For a moment Amelia and I just stood there, looking at each other.

I said, "You never ever before left a note like that. What's going on here?"

Amelia took the patient's right hand in hers and said, "This is Oscar Asch. The police have been here. Magistrate Spencer has been here."

"What the hell happened?"

"I've only seen the preliminary report. From what I can gather, there was a rally downtown. Oscar Asch was manning a table. There was a sign 'Europeans for Canada.' They were showing solidarity with our troops and raising funds. Oscar had provided bread pudding. The report suggests his accent singled him out. I don't know what that means, exactly, 'singled him out.' It was an unruly crowd, that's the word in the report. 'Unruly.' He's been stabbed twice. He's been pistol whipped. Two others from the same incident are in hospital here. They will survive."

"And Oscar Asch?"

"Odds are definitely against. Punctured spleen and lung. Severe concussion. Internal bleeding, maybe in the brain, we don't know yet. There've been transfusions."

"Anyone arrested yet?"

"The report said assailants disappeared into the crowd."

"Is he conscious?"

"Barely. He blinks. He opens his mouth but no words come out."

"If I said something to him, would he hear it?"

"I can't say for certain."

"I'm going to tell him he has a daughter."

"Just make it about the child. Not about Elizabeth. It's more merciful."

"You're right."

"Considering it might be the last thing he hears. If he hears it."

"Of course."

"I think it's soon to be a homicide."

"How soon?"

"He's got a strong will to live. But I don't think he's long for the world, Toby. He's fading. I think hours."

And so I leaned down and, not in a whisper, told Oscar Asch, "You have a daughter." There was no register of this on his face. But I did hear him utter "Oh."

"He may well have heard it," Amelia said. "Or he might've just made that sound. He's made it before."

We sat in chairs on either side of the bed.

Amelia said, "Sometimes you get strange urges with certain patients that can't always be accounted for—with Oscar here, I had the urge to ask him what a Bavarian childhood was like. Like I said, it can't really be accounted for. Some random curiosity just leaps to mind."

Mary Origo brought in two cups of coffee. We sipped our coffee and sat saying nothing. An hour went by.

"Would you feel you've abandoned a patient if we went home?" I said.

"You know, I only recognized his name because you mentioned it so often. Imagine my surprise. But my shift's long over, darling."

"All right then. Let's go home."

"I'll ask John Garvin to drive us. He's sometimes an orderly, sometimes this, that, or the other thing. We like each other. He'll just go on break."

John Garvin dropped us off and we more or less stumbled into the house.

In the kitchen Amelia said, "I'm wrung out."

Upstairs we put on nightshirts and crawled into bed.

"Did you ever think about how busy a day in the Old Testament was?" I said.

"Good Lord, Toby. If I died in my sleep, is that the last thing you'd want to have said to me?"

"I love you more than life itself."

"That's better. Let's please try and sleep. Tomorrow I don't have to be at hospital till four. So at breakfast, I'm going to have curiosities. Things I didn't think to ask earlier. Things you didn't mention. For instance, at Petit-de-Grat, did you actually speak with Elizabeth Frame. Did you actually speak to Peter Lear. The child. Things you didn't mention or did only a little."

"I'll make us breakfast. Then I'll tell you."

~

NEXT DAY, by the time Amelia got to the hospital, Oscar Asch was in the morgue.

JUST TELL ME

Journal entry October 24, 1918. 1:55 a.m. Halifax

"What Gets Revealed over a Simple Lunch"
"A Change of Newspapers"
"An Exhausting Waltz"
"Oscar Asch's Recipes"

FIRST THING I WANT TO MENTION IS THAT I'VE been thinking about the accuracy and inaccuracy of memory; my journal is not stenography, nor is it newspaper writing. And I realize, of course, that unless a stenographer is present, if the intention is to preserve any given conversation, verisimilitude is the best one can hope for. Verisimilitude seems the best possible hope I have for these journal entries.

One morning about a week ago, Amelia and I had breakfast together, and then we decided to splurge and have lunch together at Hotel Drake.

Over soup and a cucumber salad, Amelia said, "We haven't seen friends in months. It occurred to me that since we both spend much of each day around lots of people, me in hospital, you when you're at the newspaper, we don't necessarily want human company outside of that. But I do miss our friends. Then there's the Spanish flu, which doesn't exactly invite dancing after dinner, does it? I suppose everyone's just trying to manage. Just to manage."

"Not that life hasn't been demanding."

"But I do miss certain friends. But I know everyone's in the same boat, what with this epidemic."

"And you've got your temporary marching orders now."

"Any subject other than the war and Spanish flu risks sounding superfluous. It makes me just want to walk into a florist's and talk about every single type of flower. Something like that."

"I'm grateful for our private subjects, though. Between us."

"You mean like Elizabeth Frame? Oh, I'm sorry I said that. I didn't mean to say that."

"I know I've put you through a lot with my . . . obsession. With Parrsboro. And now Petit-de-Grat."

"We put each of us through things. That is life just now."

"Is there something else? Just tell me."

"Toby, take a deep breath. I want to talk about that little girl up in Petit-de-Grat. I want to talk about your responsibility to her. I want to talk about that. And I want to help with it. I have ideas about this."

"What do you mean 'responsibility'?"

"You said the village physician—Dr. O'Shee—you said that he asked you to contact Oscar Asch. Well, there's no helping that now, is there. But you said he also asked you to contact Elizabeth Frame's mother. I think it's Elsbeth, if I recall correctly. I've begun to feel you are representing that little girl in the world. That little girl's mother is in the ground in Petit-de-Grat, and her father's in the Poorhouse Burying Ground on Spring Garden Road. Stripped of all mourning paraphernalia and no words said for him. I see that sort of thing every day. And I think you have to look directly at this situation. You have to size it up and act on it."

"My organized, pragmatic wife suddenly wants to enter the fray."

"I'm saying it's something we can do together. It's maybe the most unusual situation possible. Its unusualness is a little scary in a way. But it's something we can do together. I'm saying the story has gotten inside me."

"I'm surprised to hear this."

"You might better have noticed how closely I listened and imagined how it might be affecting me."

"Guilty on all counts."

"All right, so then this is what your organized, pragmatic wife has in mind: You wire the proprietor of Ottawa House and tell her of Elizabeth Frame's death and that there's a daughter. You say you're married to a physician, and in a physician's care you can deliver the child to her grandmother, Elsbeth Frame. You can't predict how this news will be received. But you can at least give it a shot."

"Bad pun, considering whose mother you are talking about."

"I'll laugh at that later, okay? Now—if you hear back in a positive way, we wait until enough time has passed, when the child can travel, right? Then we go together to Petit-de-Grat. I will be introduced to Dr. O'Shee. I can inquire of the child, you know, physician to physician. We can show him the wire from Parrsboro, if one arrives. We can then take the child to Parrsboro. And you'll have represented her as fully as possible in the world, see what I mean?"

"I think it's a good plan."

"If it goes as planned, sure."

I GAVE AMELIA'S PLAN A LOT OF THOUGHT, and not just insomnia thought, either, but pretty much day and night. How does a person fully comprehend exactly what they think is occurring in a life—where's Heraclitus when I need him? I'm only half kidding here. If it were possible to love Amelia even more, I did so after our lunch conversation. Walking with her to the hospital, we said nothing. But when we arrived there she said, "I keep thinking, that little girl, it's not her fault, the circumstances of her birth. Not her fault, I keep thinking. Not her fault."

To put it directly as possible, Amelia's convictions are forces of nature; this one was no exception. I stopped by the Tired Monks Café and got a coffee. Directly from the café, I sent the wire to Josephine Huntley from the *Evening Mail*.

~

I SPENT A NUMBER OF DAYS working on what I privately called "Elizabeth's Story." I pretty much stuck to the actual chronology; after all, I was writing for readers of a newspaper, not readers of a novel, where chronology might take second place to sheer momentum and incident. The hearing. Elizabeth going on the lam. Her death in Petit-de-Grat (which I described in very few details—what if someday the child reads the article that some adult in Parrsboro has put in a drawer? The thought did occur to me. What if the child were raised with a different story of her parents, a story with—how to put it? ... a kinder perspective than the truth?). I made only passing mention of Peter Lear. Borrowing some words from Magistrate Spencer, I wrote that I never fully understood Lear's design in going on the lam with Elizabeth Frame. "Somewhat mysterious was her travel companion, one Peter Lear, the stenographer originally assigned to the hearing. His designs on a fugitive existence with Elizabeth Frame remain, to this reporter, elusive." Still, I think I told a good newspaper human interest story, arguably the sort you don't often hear, and

I brushed a shellac of tragedy over it all, on purpose. Even though I left out the child altogether.

The morning I finished typing out the story, I walked it over to the *Evening Standard* and got an immediate audience with Homer Orlen. Homer has a booming intellect, a large redheaded fellow. He was using a typewriter.

"Yes, I type loud as a woodpecker!" he said with an outsized laugh. He reached out to shake hands. His vise grip just seemed absentminded, not with any intent to impress. "Toby Havenshaw, good to finally meet you," he said. "What have you got there?"

"Give it a read," I said. "If you want it, it's yours."

"Why not go next door and get a coffee. It's a quiet café."

"Fine."

"Come back in an hour."

When I sat across from his desk again, Homer said, "There's a few sentences too high up in the atmosphere. I've taken a pencil to those. Me being editor in chief and all. And—and this is a word I'm almost embarrassed to use—your piece is a little too *creative*. On the other hand, it's unusual. And unusual sells newspapers, along with the usual. And I think this story of yours will sell papers. Let me ask you something, though."

"Please."

"Do you consider this a job application?"

"Yes, most definitely."

"Well, there's no love lost between Albanie Musgrave and myself, so I don't give a shit. Allow me to say, your coming to the *Standard* is a dream come true. Mrs. Courteney, editor of our matrimonial page, won't get a hotel room with me. But my *second best* wish, is you writing for us."

"Happy to hear that."

"Tell me, how do you see us presenting this unusual piece of reporting?"

"Sort of like a triptych."

"Sort of like a what?"

"Triptych. It comes from painting—a painting that's made up of three panels, and they're separate but at the same time all of a piece."

"But this is a newspaper, not an atelier. My French pronunciation is lacking."

"I just meant I see it in three parts."

"Fine. We can run it Friday, Saturday, and Sunday. After I go through it again. How's that sound?"

"It sounds good."

"By the by, you should know that in general I consider an adjective a hot air balloon. In your writing for us, try to avoid going up in hot air balloons, please."

"I'd prefer to not say anything to Albanie and wait till she sees my byline in the *Standard*."

"I'll find out where she's having lunch on publication day and book a table there for me."

We shook hands again. On the street, squeezing my hand open and shut, I thought, When you get home, better take an aspirin. I'd just changed newspapers.

⌣

AMELIA HAS PRACTICALLY BEEN LIVING in the hospital. It seems like we've scarcely seen each other. In fact, all weekend we passed like ships in the night. But finally we had dinner at

Haliburton House Inn. She wanted to celebrate the reception of my three-part story in the *Standard*, but as much as anything, she felt vindicated in her opinion of Albanie Musgrave, and she was right out front about that. The title (Part 1, Part 2, Part 3) was "A Fugitive's Life Burns Out Quietly."

As we clinked wineglasses, Amelia said, "Everyone at the hospital is talking about it. Congratulations."

"You were good and right. I needed to get away from the *Evening Mail*. So thank you."

"We've had far, far fewer nights together than I like and need. I'm so sorry. It just all can seem too much. Yesterday a gunshot wound from a fracas on the Halifax–Dartmouth ferry. Today I took out three appendixes. Three! Plus which, I read only half a page of a novel between surgeries. What sort of life is this?"

"You don't have symptoms. I don't have symptoms. A lucky life."

"Lately for you, philosophically speaking, it seems the cup's half full, darling. But lately for me, the cup's half empty."

"Either way, we're compatible." We laughed and filled our glasses again.

"Still no wire from Josephine Huntley."

"Oh my Lord, it almost slipped my mind." Amelia reached into her handbag and produced a wire. "It arrived just as I left hospital."

ELSBETH FRAME WANTS TO MEET HER GRANDDAUGHTER
STOP YOU WOULD BE IN GOD'S GOOD GRACES TO BRING
HER HERE STOP IF POSSIBLE MAKE DATE OF ARRIVAL
IN TEN DAYS EARLIEST STOP JOSEPHINE HUNTLEY STOP
OTTAWA HOUSE

"The timing is perfect, Toby," Amelia said. "More than enough time has passed so the child will be able to travel, according to Dr. O'Shee, right?"

"We don't even know if she's survived."

"Perish the thought that she hasn't. But it crossed my mind, too, naturally."

"Somehow I think Peter Lear would have informed me of that. He has my card."

"I did have a thought about Oscar Asch."

"Tell me."

"You said your impression was of an educated man. He probably has books. I was thinking that someday his daughter should know which books her father owned and read."

"You think we should somehow get some of Oscar's books as keepsakes."

"Yes, I do. I'm convinced this is important. I have only two books from my father, and I really wish I had more."

"My old contacts with the police might help with that."

"Let's get another bottle of wine."

"Sounds good to me."

"I might become a loose woman. We might have to get a room upstairs, right here in Haliburton House Inn."

However, we eventually made it home. It proved almost entirely to be a sleepless night. But for reasons other than insomnia.

⁓

SOME DAYS LATER I again spoke with Magistrate Spencer in his office.

"Your piece in the *Standard* skimmed right over Peter Lear," he said. "I didn't much care. He made his bed and has to sleep in it every night for the rest of his life."

"So nobody's going to go after him?"

"Not likely. Mr. Havenshaw—in case you hadn't noticed, there's a war going on. Every outport in Nova Scotia has the potential to become Petit-de-Grat, Spanish flu-wise. In that light—and it's the light I choose to read this by—Lear is no longer a person of interest. He's a waste of taxpayers' money. He was for a short time a person of interest. He no longer is. He's a file now. There's dates on the file. He's become those dates. In your piece for the *Standard*, you yourself could have given Peter Lear more of his life back, but you choose to hardly mention him."

"He wasn't very *original* to you, anyway."

He didn't take kindly to that comment. He reached into his desk drawer, took out the revolver Elizabeth used to murder Everett Dewis, and pointed it right at me. "My secretary will see you out," he said.

⁓

I WENT DIRECTLY TO SEE HOMER ORLEN. "Before I settle in working for you," I said, "I need a few weeks away with my wife. She's been worn threadbare at her hospital." I explained the situation a little more.

"Take the time to come up with a feature," Homer said. "I want you to start on it within a month, though. That's a special dispensation and leeway I'm not known for. Keep it between us. Some of my hard-core veteran reporters might sulk. I don't want to endure their smirks, just if I go in to get a coffee in the coffee room. I'm betting on you right out of the gate, Havenshaw. But then again, your piece on the fugitive murderer sold papers like nothing I'd seen in quite a while."

"I've got a lot of thinking to do on my piece about sleeplessness."

"At least tell me a little more."

"It's early days with this. But it'd have both a psychological angle and a medical angle, and other angles. I'd interview all walks of life around Halifax. And I'd venture out into the province. I've mainly taken mental notes so far. But I even have a book about the subject in mind."

"Say, I've written two books myself. Detective novels. I've got copies around here somewhere. Interested?"

"Definitely, but when Amelia and I get back to town."

"From the sound of it, your piece could have originality. I know a whole bunch of people who can't sleep. Should you need some names. Very accomplished people, too."

"I'll take you up on that."

"I don't want smirks, Havenshaw."

"I understand."

"You're a professional. Of course you understand."

~

I'D EXPECTED A LOT OF RESISTANCE when I inquired as to the possibility of going into Oscar Asch's apartment, but much to my surprise, I encountered none at all, really. I'd so despised the thought of asking Sergeant Harnes for a favor that I fell back on what I considered the lesser of two evils: asking Magistrate Spencer for assistance.

"You mentioned me favorably in your piece in the *Standard*," he said. "And I had an assistant go through it with a fine-toothed comb. So I'll help you out here."

I should have left well enough alone, but said, "And had you found a sentence you didn't approve of?"

"Probably I would've authored my own version of Elizabeth Frame's sordid tale, and given it to Albanie Musgrave. It would have caused a dustup."

"Anyway, thanks for your help."

"I can arrange permission within the hour."

"I just want to take a few books from Oscar's apartment. Keepsakes for his daughter. The daughter you know about."

"That sort of sentimentality isn't my cup of tea. Then again, I don't have children."

"Please understand, I'm telling you straight out, that I will be taking books from the apartment. I don't want your assistance to be aiding and abetting theft."

"Thoughtful of you, Mr. Havenshaw. Take as many goddamn books as you want."

That ended that conversation.

⁓

JUST AFTER 2 P.M. Amelia and I met an Officer Mickel out front of 118 Kane Street. There was police tape festooned across his apartment's door.

"Is this a crime scene?" I asked.

"Rumor it's something to do with the Sedition Act," Officer Mickel said. "But I've been warned you used to write for the crime page. That you'd be nosy. So no more questions, okay?"

I had the thought that the police might attempt to smear

Oscar Asch's reputation in retrospect. Blame the victim, as it were. He'd years ago been investigated for the Sedition Act and cleared, so why now again? Could they be so stupid or conniving as to try and make it seem that his table full of free bread pudding was actually just putting a smile on devious intent? If you work for a newspaper long enough—and this might be especially true of wartime—anything you might imagine people doing, they've done it. Or will do it. The Halifax police were no exception.

When Officer Mickel said what he'd said, Amelia threw me a look: *Don't rock the boat.* We had a simple task: Don't complicate things.

Amelia said, "Look at the bookshelves!" Her outsized sense of delight persuaded Officer Mickel to shut the door behind him and wait out in the hallway.

Oscar's apartment had four rooms: dining room, small kitchen, library, and bedroom, where the floor-to-ceiling bookshelves were. Though there were stacks of books in every room. The piano was in the dining room. It all felt like intellectual life spilled over. Sheet music was stacked on the dining room table and in columns along the dining room wall. There was a ledger, which I opened; it contained a calendar of lessons and appointments. Paging through, I saw that in at least half a dozen places, the name *Elizabeth Frame* had been crudely circled in red, no doubt by the police, though they clearly had no more use for the ledger itself. Also circled in red was the name *Ursula Müller*— probably because it was a German name. Perhaps that and that alone. Next to this name Oscar had written: *Seriously gifted. Writing a piece worthy of Chopin.* Next to one entry for Elizabeth, Oscar had written: *Curious large enthusiasms. At present, possibly more dedicated to letters about composition than composition itself. We shall see.*

Amelia picked up a notebook from the kitchen counter and paged through it. Holding up the notebook for me to see, she said, "Toby, it's all recipes!" She put the notebook into her handbag, straight-out theft, but at this point, what did it matter?

Amelia walked into the bedroom and perused the bookshelves. I was sitting on the piano bench.

"Only about one out of ten of these books are in English," she said. "The rest are in German, except for some in Dutch, and some in French, and at least two in Russian."

"Here I'm Canadian and I have trouble with English."

Amelia stepped from the bedroom holding three thick volumes. "As far as I can make out, the German is mostly philosophy," she said. "Some of the French are novels. Victor Hugo."

"Let's just say the child's raised in Parrsboro."

"Yes, books in English would suffice. But it wouldn't give her the full idea of who Oscar was, would it? Keepsakes need to fully represent her father. So definitely we'll take a few in German."

"German philosophers sound about right."

"I think that a few of his foreign cookbooks would be important for the child. Cooking was one of Oscar's interests in life, you see."

"It all makes sense to me. Should we go?"

"Don't hurry me, Toby. This requires some thought. I can see how uncomfortable you are right now. But it takes some thought."

In a short while, Amelia settled on ten books plus four cookbooks.

"I'm also a little uncomfortable suddenly," she said. "Are we robbing the dead for some idea of what's right? I mean, how can we know?"

"From the get-go I thought it was a good idea. To think that far ahead on behalf of a child you've never even seen."

But Amelia looked on the verge of tears. "All day I see things I should cry over but don't," she said. "Not professional, you see. But here right now. In this apartment. In this ugly part of the city, but this nicely appointed apartment, the heart feels at cross-purposes—thank you, Mr. Heraclitus, for that way of putting it. Not to mention I saw Oscar Asch when he was first admitted to hospital, didn't I. Plus which, those lovely watercolor paintings on the wall there. Who might have painted those? I don't know what I'm trying to say."

The books were now stacked on the piano. Amelia walked to the phonograph on its stand. She took a record album from its sheath and placed it on the turntable, cranked up the phonograph, and we heard it was a waltz. Amelia held out her arms to me.

"Neither of us know how to waltz," she said. "But so what? Let the sad Bavarian ghost see us try."

"I don't sense a ghost here."

"I do."

We kept to the small space of the dining room, then moved awkwardly, but holding each other tightly, into the bedroom and out again, and then as if on cue we abruptly stopped.

The door suddenly opened and Officer Mickel said, "Time to leave now."

"You might think you know what you just saw," Amelia said, "but you're too young to know anything."

Amelia picked up the cookbooks and four other books, and I picked up the rest and followed her to the open door.

Amelia stopped and turned and said, "Officer, do you want a list of the books we've taken? For the record? Just to show your competence?"

"My understanding is," Mickel said, "nobody cares one way or the other." He put the record back in its sheath and turned off the phonograph machine.

When we all three stood out front of the building, Officer Mickel said, "I've got transportation from the police pool. I'm instructed to drive you home."

"Full service," Amelia said. "How nice."

⁓

ONCE WE WERE BACK in our own house, we placed the books on the kitchen table and Amelia set the notebook of recipes on the kitchen counter.

"I think a brandy is in order now," Amelia said.

"It's only four thirty."

"It's just a response to being in Oscar's apartment. Besides, I already did rounds this morning, and my next surgery isn't until six a.m. tomorrow. I'm going to jot down the German book titles. My colleague Dr. Freiberg is fluent. He'll provide the translations, I'm quite sure. I can then write the title in English under the German on each title page."

I moved the books to the guest bedroom. Dinner at the kitchen table was haddock and potatoes roasted with olive oil and oregano, with a spritz of garlic and lemon juice.

Amelia was paging through Oscar's recipes. "I'm definitely going to give some of these a try," she said.

"Well, you tried to save his life. The least he could do is give you some recipes."

"A little sanctimonious, don't you think? I tried to save his life because he came in on a gurney. I just want to know how some of these recipes actually taste. Listen to this one, for instance." She read the recipe for something called *Pichelsteiner Stew*, which had lamb, beef, carrots, leeks, parsnips, and more.

"Sounds delicious," I said.

"But we can't have it with cheap wine. No sir. We'll need to buy an expensive bottle. Maybe from France."

"We can raise a glass to Oscar Asch."

"No, having his recipes is quite enough. In my opinion it's quite enough. Otherwise, I'd prefer to keep Oscar Asch out of our kitchen, let alone a candlelight dinner."

"What was I thinking?"

"I get the sentiment, though. I can get too close to a patient, rarely but now and again. I've found it's best to choose a distance to keep and keep it."

More brandy after dinner made us sleepy, and we lay down on our bed and slept the entire night in our clothes. When I woke, Amelia had already left for the hospital. She had left a note on the kitchen table: *An exhausting waltz—lugging German philosophy books into our house—brandy—good Lord, what a woman will go through just for a good night's sleep. I'll get coffee at hospital. You'll have to make your own. In this peculiar life of late, I love you even more.*

A PEACEFUL CHILD

Journal entry November 16, 1918. 5:15 a.m. Halifax

"Back to Petit-de-Grat"
"Back to Parrsboro"
"On to Advocate Harbor"

I SENT A RETURN WIRE AND SET THE DATE WITH Elsbeth Frame, with Josephine Huntley as intermediary. In the meantime, there was much to attend to. Amelia had to coordinate her leave of absence with the other surgeons; all sorts of details had to be worked out there. With help from the pediatrics staff, Amelia arranged for diapers, baby powder, this and that, and she followed everyone's advice in such matters, though she fibbed and told them, "I'm to take care of a friend's baby for a short while." She even purchased some infant pajamas and other clothes. "We'll be amateurs at all of this," she said to me. "Learn as we go, but after all, it's only for a day or so."

I had to work up a proposal for my three-part investigation into sleeplessness, which Homer told me would, upon approval, run in successive Sunday editions.

When I showed Homer a rough of the proposal, he said, "Just go ahead and work on it. When you hand it in, then the real fun begins."

"But the concept of it—what do you think?"

"I don't think in terms of *concepts*. That's a professor's word. I just read what's written and step into a reader's shoes. Seeing as I'm paying you so well, I need to trust in my investment, you see. The piece you wrote on the fugitives was straight-out good human interest stuff. Plus it got talked about."

"You worried that sleeplessness isn't a newspaper subject?"

"If I allow it in the *Standard*, it's a newspaper subject. But with this sleeplessness thing, what about that woman—did you hear about her? That woman in Peggy's Cove who claims she hasn't slept in a decade, and every night sees her long-deceased sister and her long-deceased husband walking hand in hand along the seawall. I guess that's the kind of thing you meant when you said 'psychological angle.'"

"I had in mind something more pedestrian. But I'll look into her."

We shook hands and I left Homer's office. My hand ached right away. I thought, He's a fellow who doesn't know his own strength, or maybe he knows it all too well. I'd heard that Homer was once invited to speak to a journalism class at Dalhousie University. By the time he was through, he'd convinced all but two students to go into different professions. The professor who'd invited Homer begged off lunch with him.

⁓

AMELIA CONTINUED WITH HER SURGERIES. The night before we left for Petit-de-Grat, we talked at the kitchen table and she said, "Well, tomorrow we're off to a once-in-a-lifetime thing."

"I'm not at all sure how to think about it."

"Going to fetch the child and bring her to her grandmother? It feels the right thing to do. Who else will do it? As far as I could determine, it was either she goes to Parrsboro or to an orphanage."

"Elizabeth Frame certainly didn't have a Last Will and Testament."

"Her thoughts must've been unraveling at the end."

"I am with you in this, Amelia. Completely with you. But deep down I feel I'm still missing something essential. Essential to your wanting to get so deeply involved. It's a terrible feeling."

Amelia sighed; the moment seemed to pain her. "Seeing children die in hospital. Influenza. It makes me want to act on the side of life. I know I've said that exact thing before. We go to Petit-de-Grat. We deliver the child to her grandmother. We get some rest and recuperation—to use the military lingo—in Advocate Harbor. Maybe we even sleep well there by the sea."

"That would be nice."

"Toby, if we aren't equally committed here, I'll carry out the plan by myself. And I won't mind being in Advocate Harbor by myself, either. As you know, I'm quite resourceful."

The rest of the evening felt more like a truce. More like living side by side. Passages of such merciless civility in our marriage—and I mean even a few hours—always gave me a feeling of hopelessness. Maybe for Amelia, too. She never said.

〜

AT 4:30 A.M. WE SET OUT for Petit-de-Grat in the car provided by the hospital. I considered myself to be traveling with someone with great and clear purpose and conviction. While privately I was trying to distance myself from Elizabeth Frame, it seemed to me that what Amelia had said—"The story has gotten inside me"—*that* truth was conveying us to Petit-de-Grat.

Just like last time, the village seemed so empty. According to Amelia's medical contacts, things in this region in terms of Spanish flu had worsened. "Please let's keep our distance," she said as we stopped in front of Dr. and Mrs. O'Shee's house at about 3 p.m.

There were long flat clouds on the horizon. Once out of the car, Amelia wanted to walk down to the wharf, so we did that. There were four trawlers in harbor, *Poseidon's Weeping Mistress*, *Oceanus's Mad Wife*, *Ponto's Lonely Wife*, and *Nereus's Secluded Wife*.

"Hmm," Amelia said, "it seems the sea gods make for bad husbands here in Petit-de-Grat. But I always suspected the gods were feckless in that way. Of course, they had other strengths. And not everyone's cut out for marriage, right?"

"We're cut out for it."

"The sea air is nice."

"But pretty soon we should get set up in the church."

We stayed at the wharf for fifteen or so minutes more, and during that time *Fiddler's Woe* chugged back into harbor. I waved to Mr. Tennyson and he waved back. Then we drove to the church, unpacked some things, and made the pews as homey as possible.

"Best to eat the cold chicken out of the ice chest sooner than later," Amelia said. "There's the apple pie, too."

I set out our early dinner. "A picnic on a church pew. Who'd have ever thought."

"It's going to get chilly in here later," I said. "I speak from experience."

"I packed enough quilts and blankets for five people."

After we ate dinner, we went to Dr. and Mrs. O'Shee's house. I knocked on the door and Dr. O'Shee answered and said, "Your letter arrived with news of the child's father. I've been expecting you. As a physician, I'm responsible here for the child. I think your wanting to bring her to her grandmother is the Christian thing to do. But she'll stay in the warmth of this house until tomorrow. My wife and I will have everything ready for you in the morning. Is that understood?"

"I'm Dr. Amelia Morley," Amelia said. "I'll be taking care of the child every minute to Parrsboro."

"I'll rest assured she's in good hands, then."

"Thank you," Amelia said.

"I understand you're a surgeon."

"That's right."

"A woman on the hospital surgical staff. Things have changed. For the better, if you ask me. My wife is a trained nurse. You'll meet her tomorrow."

"I look forward to it," Amelia said.

"Well, it's getting nippy out, but I have something to say, so bear with me. When Peter Lear arrived here, he told us very straightforwardly the fix he was in. And you've seen him, Mr. Havenshaw. You've seen how wrung out he is. He's even more wrung out than when you were last here. He's lost his soul. He does not sleep. This intelligent, handsome young fellow. Mrs. O'Shee and myself, we just could not for the life of us understand what was in it for him. He had to have known from the get-go, this cannot end well. Will he go to prison?"

"No," I said. "I have that on good authority."

"Good authority sometimes changes its mind."

"True, but I think Peter Lear won't go to prison."

"He's been given a second chance, then."

"You could say that, yes."

"He told us he's going back to his family in Sydney Mines."

"Where is he now?"

"He's in the room where Elizabeth Frame died, that's where he stays. Right now he's asleep next to a bottle of spirits, bereft of any liveliness, unshaven as ever, in need of a bath. He reads his pocket diaries night and day. If he thinks his soul is going to return to him in that room, he's sadly mistaken. He's become his despair. That's my opinion, anyway. My wife feels similarly but she puts it differently."

"I take it the child is doing well."

"Sweet and beautiful child, and sleeps like an angel. I call her a strong sleeper."

"Born into a caring house. Fortunate for her."

"But you see, we don't want Peter Lear with us anymore. We just don't, and I have to say it bluntly. We've fed him for weeks. We're going to give him a little money. But he and Elizabeth brought a lot of exhaustion and peculiarity and sleeplessness into our house. Every single day was a tug-of-war. On the one hand, there's this beautiful young woman, some might say all the more beautiful for being with child, a woman with a lively turn of mind, often fanciful, almost lewdly direct. I know Mrs. O'Shee secretly enjoyed talking with her. On the other hand, blink twice, you're looking at a woman who murdered her own husband on their wedding night. Oh yes, we knew all about that. Now, once Peter Lear leaves, we'll burn the bed Elizabeth died in. To some that'd be superstition, but to Mrs. O'Shee it's required. Still, we took them in, didn't we? No one made us take them in. It might've been Christian charity. It also might have been Christian stupidity. Here's what I think: Peter Lear had better try and ask God for forgiveness and figure out how to be instructed by his regrets."

"You kept the child alive," Amelia said. "You must be a very fine physician. I agree with my husband. She was born into a caring house. I hope she's going to one, too."

Dr. O'Shee brightened a little. "Do you know, that little nameless orphan? She sleeps through the night. I don't mean every night, of course, but most every night. No matter who she was born to, that is one peaceful child."

He shut the door and we drove to the church.

WE SAT TALKING BY LANTERN LIGHT, and finally got settled best we could under blankets and quilts, and I think we both held out some hope for sleep. But then there was a loud knock at the front door of the church.

"If that's Elizabeth Frame, I'm going to pull down the cross and fight her off," Amelia said.

"I know, it's a little creepy sleeping in this church. I'm sorry."

"Please go see who our houseguest is."

When I opened the door, there was Peter Lear, holding a lantern near his face and standing at least ten meters back.

"Mr. Havenshaw," he said. "Disregard my appearance."

"You look half dead, or half alive, or something."

"I know you're here with your surgeon wife—my apologies but—"

"Come in but stay well back, please. If you're going to sit, sit across the aisle."

He followed me into the church. Amelia had a surgical mask on.

"I'm Peter Lear," he said to Amelia. "I don't have any symptoms."

"You can't always know such a thing," Amelia said. "Are you hungry? We have some apple pie left."

"No thank you," Lear said.

He sat across the aisle and halfway down the pew.

Amelia lowered her mask and said, "I'm not sure if it's a pleasure to meet you. But my husband's kept me apprised of who you are, Mr. Lear."

Peter had a winter coat on and fisherman's galoshes. He looked around the church. "Maybe the Spanish flu might be afraid to come in here," he said.

"Wishful thinking," Amelia said.

"I know my reputation precedes me, Dr. Morley," Lear said, "but your husband was cordial to me in Parrsboro. I knew he was a newspaper reporter, but still and all, he was cordial to me. And he saw things through Dr. and Mrs. O'Shee's window, I'm sure he's told you. And I've read the piece he wrote about Elizabeth Frame—that article made its way here and I read it. And Dr. O'Shee told me of your letter to him and what's going to happen now to the child."

"You've got a tough road ahead," I said. "But say what you need to say."

"About those transcripts. They were only the one side, you see. Elizabeth's side is what you read. But she wanted to know things about me, too. It wasn't as if I was only the stenographer."

"Peter, what the hell happened with you? In Parrsboro."

"Something got set in motion."

"But after that, any point along the way, you could have come to your senses."

"It was a courtship of sorts."

"Not by any definition I've ever heard."

"It was a courtship with a hopeless beginning and a hope-less end. A reckless beginning. An illegal beginning. With a life together impossible no matter what the end."

"Elizabeth told you she was heading to see Oscar Asch. It says so in the transcript."

"Well, it's the only courtship I ever had."

There was a long silence.

"As I see it," Peter said, "the sooner I can put my pocket diaries to good use, the better."

"You want to start visiting the bereaved families, is that it?"

"The families and wives and sons and daughters from the pocket diaries, yes."

"I wish you all good luck. You realize you'll cause both pain and solace."

"Privately, I know I'm intelligent. Publicly, when I go home to Sydney Mines, I'll almost certainly be seen as a laughingstock. My parents won't want to be seen with me in church."

"Have they seen you since you got back from France?" Amelia said.

"No."

"On that account, don't you think they'll be so pleased?" Amelia said.

"I'm not so sure. I know them. I know how I was raised."

"Your being in France will have to count for something," I said.

"What I did since coming back will erase that, I think."

"It might not."

"Do you think the authorities have been to speak to my parents in their house?"

"Yes," I said.

"Do you think the authorities will come for me?"

"No."

"I'm going to start visiting bereaved families. I'll clean myself up."

"That'll give you purpose," Amelia said.

"I think I'll sell my stenographic machine. Nobody's going to hire me in Nova Scotia, are they?"

"Doubtful," I said. "I'll buy the machine from you."

"Why would you do that?"

"I'll pay for a lesson or two on it. I'll find somebody for that. I can use it for some of my future interviews."

"Interviews for the crime page?"

"I've changed course. Do you want to sell it to me or not?"

"It cost me fifty-five dollars. It's yours for twenty."

"I have that much in my wallet."

"Fair enough. When you come to get the child tomorrow, I'll have it waiting."

I handed him twenty dollars.

"I'll be going now. Thanks for inviting me in."

When he stood up, I said, "Did you originally write *moons*, or did you write *moans*?"

He faced toward the church door. He said nothing for a good full minute. Without looking at me or Amelia, he said, "I originally wrote *moons*. I think *moans* was just too much for me."

"Whether or not I see you tomorrow, good luck," I said.

"Luck is for fishing. As it now stands, with my situation. Improvement will take divine intervention."

⁓

ABOUT NINE O'CLOCK the next morning, with Dr. O'Shee and Peter Lear nowhere in sight, Mrs. O'Shee handed Amelia the

swaddled child and said, "The machine is there on the porch."
She simply turned around and went back inside her house.
So with Amelia holding the child and me holding the steno-
graphic machine, we got into the touring car. We drove out of
Petit-de-Grat.

"See any ghosts chasing in the rearview?" Amelia said.

"There you go again," I said.

"I just think this lovely child should make a clean getaway."

The world opened up before us, a sunny day with no clouds to
speak of, an extra container of gasoline well secured in the trunk,
in a way that it wouldn't budge even on a rough stretch of road.
Parrsboro was about 313 kilometers.

If I drove, Amelia held the child, and when we switched drivers,
I held her. I remember we reprised, in as much detail and laughter
as possible, our honeymoon in Scotland, everything from seasick-
ness to Amelia's aunts, uncles, and cousins, and a house rented for
three days on a cliff by the sea, the meals we cooked there. But on
our way to Parrsboro, mainly we were in the moment with the
child, every expression, hiccup, every moment of the miracle of
sleep. We had rubber nipples that Mrs. O'Shee had sterilized in
boiling water, and we had many bottles of Mellin's evaporated
milk. Just at dusk we got set up in room 101 in Gillespie House
Inn. We got wood burning in the fireplace. We were exhausted.

But we hadn't been there for more than fifteen or so minutes
when there was a knock on the door. When I opened it, there,
standing at a safe distance, stood Rector Shrevard.

"Please keep your distance," Amelia said.

"This is my wife, Dr. Morley," I said.

"I'm Rector Shrevard. St. George's Anglican Church. Nice to
make your acquaintance."

Amelia didn't respond. I said, "To what do we owe the pleasure?"

"Elsbeth Frame is quarantined with Spanish flu," he said. "So is Josephine Huntley, who is not quite as ill—she informed me of the approximate date of your arrival and I've judiciously checked Gillespie House. All told, in Parrsboro we have eighteen ill. None have yet gone to their reward. Dr. Particulate is living on coffee, as it were. Bravely attending. My strongest best advice to you is, try to get a good night's sleep and leave first thing in the morning. The child included, temporarily. There's no one capable of taking in the child just now. Later we can contact you in the city."

"What, if anything, has your Dr. Particulate said about Elsbeth Frame's condition?" Amelia said. She was sitting on the bed holding the child.

"He won't traffic in predictions," Rector Shrevard said.

"This is some turn of events," I said.

"Everyone's got troubles everywhere," Shrevard said.

"My husband and I were on our way to Advocate Harbor," Amelia said. "We're quite tired now. Thank you for this lovely room."

"I'll see that sandwiches are set outside your door." Amelia held up a container of Mellin's evaporated milk. Rector Shrevard immediately said, "Oh, of course. I'll see to it that two dozen are sent over from the all-purpose."

"Greatly appreciated, thank you," Amelia said.

"It'll come out of the church coffers."

⌇

WHEN SHREVARD LEFT, Amelia bathed the child in the bathtub down the hall. She brought her back to our room, then walked down the hall for her own bath. When she returned, she said, "These were outside the door." She brought in a picnic basket; inside were muffins, sandwiches, a thermos of coffee. The Mellin's evaporated milk was in a separate box. Amelia leaned down to the bed and pressed her lips to the child's forehead. "No symptoms," she said. "Little one, good for you." Amelia warmed a bottle of milk by the fire, tested the milk, then let the child have as much as she wanted.

"I see only one choice here," she said. "On to Advocate Harbor. Two weeks there, with the three of us, suddenly offers us something."

"What might that be?"

"You've stopped writing about murder. I'm away from the hospital. For two weeks, we'll at least be with new life. I've really come to like that phrase, 'new life,' haven't I."

"I see the cup's half full again for you."

"Possibly. A day at a time, my darling." She nuzzled the child's nose. "A day at a time, a day at a time, a day at a time."

⌒

FROM PARRSBORO WE CONTINUED ON to Advocate Harbor. With the child in tow, Amelia and I didn't quite know what we'd become. We were at once striving and perplexed in our capacity as surrogate parents, if that's the right word for what we were. It seemed we were running on unpracticed emotions.

At one point Amelia said, "I'll just say it. I'm glad we have her with us. I'm sorry nobody wanted her in Parrsboro. Not yet at least. But I'm not sorry we have her with us."

"I'm not sorry either."

The cottage was about fifty meters up from the beach. It was cozy and welcoming; there was dried driftwood next to the fireplace. Early afternoon, the three of us bundled up, we set out for the beach. It was cold but sunny. I held the child. Amelia said, "Let's wait until well into next year to try and understand 1918." I knew exactly what she meant; too much had happened. Over the week, we cooked and slept, we took care of the child. "What are we here?" Amelia said. "How should we think of ourselves with this little orphan girl?" We both were all questions and no answers, which proved a kind of rhetoric of discovery, because it got us thinking.

The child woke us up crying on only five nights. Each day we took a walk. Four or five times I drove to a nearby store for cereal and milk and fish for dinner, but mostly we stayed in or near the cottage. One day we took hoes and a shovel and turned over the earth in the winter garden. We collected driftwood and dried it by the driftwood fire. Amelia had brought along no medical journals. In pillow talk, when I told her I'd filled three notebooks about sleeplessness, she said, "'He left behind a life reporting on murder and wrote a book.' That holds out some promise as an epitaph, if you ask me." Some evenings, once the child was asleep, we'd each have a glass of brandy. One night in particular, we surprised ourselves with a new amorousness. We remained absent of symptoms. The Bay of Fundy delivered no storms. I must admit, all in all, the time isolated at the far sequestered end of the province was a reprieve from all ghastly things. How long had it been since Amelia and I had had such a constancy of days and nights together, but of course figure in the child. Of course, we didn't feel we could give her a name, not even a nickname. That wasn't up to us.

Then, after dinner on our last evening in the cottage, while reading *The Magnificent Ambersons*, Amelia fell asleep in the overstuffed chair near the fireplace. She had a blanket across her lap. Opposite Amelia, the child was tucked in asleep in the crib we'd discovered in a storage room. I was lying on the sofa, reading a year-old copy of the *Canadian Magazine* that perhaps Bethany Bates had left behind. I came across a Q&A with L. M. Montgomery. The eighth question presented to her was, "Do you remember your first public reading of *Anne of Green Gables*?" The answer she gave was: "Oh, so many years ago! But I believe it was 1908, when the book was first published. I'd been invited to the small village of Parrsboro, Nova Scotia. It's all a little hazy now. But I distinctly recall that after my presentation at the Anglican Girls' School, a woman more or less pushed her daughter forward. And much to my astonishment, this precocious daughter recited the entirety of 'Dover Beach' by Matthew Arnold. Do you know the poem? It's much too long for our present purposes. But it begins,

The sea is calm tonight. / The tide is full, the moon lies fair / Upon the straits; on the French coast, the light / Gleams and is gone; the cliffs of England stand / Glimmering and vast, out in the tranquil bay. / Come to the window, sweet is the night-air!"

I heard myself gasp. I knew the daughter pushed forward by her mother had to have been fourteen-year-old Elizabeth Frame. It was the most haunting revelation imaginable. *Come to the window.* It shook me to the core. I decided to take the magazine; I'd eventually find the right time to show it to Amelia.

OUR FINAL MORNING AT THE COTTAGE, Amelia and I bathed and fed the child and bundled her up for the return travel. For some reason Amelia took the stethoscope from her doctor's bag and listened to the child's heart. "All's right with you," she said. "All's good." We breakfasted on coffee and toast, scrubbed clean the dishes, tidied up the rooms, packed and carried our travel bags to the touring car. It was a blustery day; if you went by the activity of clouds and waves building, the bay seemed to be changing its temperament.

I quickly warmed up the car. Then Amelia and the child got into the passenger side. Right away Amelia discovered, tucked into the holder on the passenger-side door, a folded special edition of the *Truro Weekly News*. I suspected it was Colleen North, neighbor and caretaker of the cottage, whom we'd met on our second day—she'd left the paper because she so rightly thought we'd want to know. With the car idling, Amelia, somewhat breathless, read the headlines out loud: " 'Fighting Ends at Six A.M.' 'Kaiser Flees to Holland.' " We could scarcely believe it. Amelia spoke first to the child: "Just a few weeks old and your first war ended. I'm so happy for you." As we sat in the car, the slightly noisy heater keeping us warm, I now held the child as Amelia read paragraph after paragraph, three full pages in all. Names of battles. Unfathomable statistics of dead and wounded and missing. The conditions of surrender. On page four, obituaries of soldiers who'd lived in or near Truro. Finally, Amelia let the paper fall away to the floor, sighed deeply and said, "Sure, this is written in good clear sentences. But to me what's needed is a requiem." But I thought, Well at least there were direct quotes from soldiers and widows. Which made for urgent language.

Just a few minutes out of Advocate Harbor, Amelia said, "I've a mind to turn right around and unpack in the cottage."

"I know what you mean."

"So now we go to find out if Elsbeth Frame is still with us."

Of course, the breathtaking news of the Armistice was on our minds. We had Elizabeth and Oscar's daughter in our care: the wider world, and the world close-up. And soon just up ahead, the outport of Parrsboro, which I'd come to associate with violent incidents. I didn't really want to stop there.

As we entered the village, Amelia said, "Before we go find Elsbeth Frame, I'd like to see where the whale washed up."

"A surprising request."

"It's not a request. I'm going to see where the whale was."

I steered the car toward the wharf, just moments away.

"Toby, I've looked at that photograph every single day—for how many months now? I've seen you bent over it like a monk. It's tacked above your trusty typewriter. I just want to see for myself."

I parked near the wooden pilings. "Right down there," I said. "Tide's out."

Amelia handed me the child and got out of the car and walked down to the beach. There were a few gulls whirling about. There was no boat in the harbor. I watched as Amelia looked out across the brooding sea. I watched as she stood where the whale had been. Then she turned and stared up toward Ottawa House. This perhaps was not in my beloved Amelia's mind in the way I thought it was, but I imagined her to be, out of private need, verifying what I'd described to her in such detail. What had

occurred here. What the photograph both depicted and represented. I was a little taken aback when Amelia then sat down on
the beach. She sat there, collar pulled up, scarf readjusted, and I
thought, Whatever meaning and effect this has for her, just let it
happen and don't ask.

When Amelia got back into the car, she took the child in
her arms and I said, "I think it's time to put that photograph in
a drawer."

I steered the car up into the village.

"Look there!" Amelia said. "Signs of life!"

There were people entering the church. Fifty or so meters away,
we sat in the idling car until everyone had disappeared inside.

"Go and see," Amelia said. "You can ask someone about Elsbeth Frame. But keep your distance, please. We've got precious
cargo with us, right?"

With Amelia and the child warm in the car, I approached
the church. I opened the door and stepped just inside, sight
unseen, I was pretty sure. There, between the front pew and
the raised pulpit, a long table had been set with plates, uten-
sils, glasses, plates of food running the length of the table. There
were perhaps twenty people in attendance; decidedly not people
in the horrid grip of Spanish flu, or seemingly much worried
about proximity.

Holding a glass of wine midair, Rector Shrevard made a
toast: "Happy birthday to you, Elsbeth. Out of a dread year,
happy birthday. Out of dark clouds passing, happy birthday. You
have gone through some of the worst life can offer. But here you
are with us. Dear old friends and neighbors, who helped see you
through. Especially Josephine, sitting right here next to you."

I recognized Dr. Particulate. I recognized Petrus Dollard.

Glasses were raised. Then everyone tucked into their food. There was a birthday cake with candles front and center on the table.

When I got in behind the steering wheel, Amelia said, "Well?"

"Clearly Elsbeth Frame changed her mind."

"Did she say that?"

"I didn't speak to anyone. It was a birthday party for her. Cake and all."

"Not only in just two weeks' time did she not perish, but she got a year older."

"But why the goddamn charade?" I drove the car through the village. "Why did Shrevard come and lie to us? Why did he use Spanish flu to put the fear of God in us, to make it seem the whole village was a threat to the child? Why such an effort toward us well-meaning people? And him a clergyman. I'm fuming."

"Desperate measures. Maybe Elsbeth was afraid of seeing her granddaughter. Maybe realizing she could never really feel like a true granddaughter. You don't hold a child, the child's not real to you."

"But she knew the child's an *orphan*. Because our wire said so. How much more real can you get?"

As we gained the road along the Bay of Fundy outside the village, I said, "I feel like turning right around and telling those people what they are."

"Being self-righteous in their own church might not work, my darling."

"I feel like going back."

"I cast my vote no to that. Unless you think you can filch a piece of birthday cake for us." All right, some levity there. "Please don't lose any sleep over this. I'd say the writing's on the wall with Elsbeth Frame. But if you do lose sleep over it, maybe it can be research for your book. You can use it. You can write how a poisonous betrayal and abandonment of an orphan child can keep a well-meaning, ethical person awake to all hours."

"I'm not in an equivocating mood. But thank you for trying, anyway."

"In time, their motives might be seen in a different light."

"I doubt it."

"I doubt it too. And if you want me to never forgive those folks, I won't forgive them."

I cracked my window slightly and we could hear seagulls.

"Well, at least we've postponed the child from being raised by heathens," I said.

"Heathens might be a bit much—the church is well kept."

"I'm fuming."

"We have to look at it straight on, Toby. Elsbeth Frame didn't want the child. Nobody there wanted the child. It's both awful and humanly understandable. There, your pragmatic wife's had her say on the matter."

"When I was first in Parrsboro for the hearing, I met some good and friendly people."

"Bad luck can change a place."

"I know you're not trying to make excuses for them, but it sounds a little like you are."

"Here's two facts I know for certain: They don't want the child. We have been living with the child and are taking her to Halifax. I can't think past these two facts just now."

"Okay, let's stop talking about it, then."

Amelia took my right hand in her left hand. "No, let's talk this thing through, or at least as far as we possibly can. Driving slow's the idea. It's a soporific for the child. And soon enough we'll be home."

~

IN FACT, THAT NIGHT we got back to Halifax at around ten or ten thirty; approaching the city, we saw fireworks out over the harbor. Once inside our house, we got the child settled in the guest room. We built a moat of quilts and blankets, so there was no possible way she could roll off the bed. In a couple of hours, she woke needing her diaper changed, and to be fed, and to be comforted, but quite soon she fell back asleep. However, for Amelia and me, the Armistice celebration that rang from the streets clearly was going to make for us a sleepless night. Out our rowhouse window we could see a stuffed life-size effigy of Kaiser Wilhelm dangling from a clothesline stretched between opposite lampposts.

At 5 a.m. we sat in pajamas and robes, drinking coffee at the kitchen table. The orderly who knocked on our door at 5:30, the very same John Garvin, said, "Dr. Morley, you're needed right away. It's a soldier debarked from the RMS *Aquitania*, come in late last night. He's in a bad way." Amelia hurriedly got dressed.

"It's a madhouse out there, Dr. Morley," Garvin said. "I'll stay close. We'll get to hospital in quick order."

"You'll be all right with our guest?" Amelia said to me. I figured she'd said "guest" to avoid giving Garvin hospital gossip.

"I'm just fine," I said. "We get along just fine."

Amelia put on her coat and scarf. I watched her set out to try and save a life. I didn't quite know how to countenance this, but in the moment, it must have been, out in the streets, the riotous density of human joyfulness that set me on edge. Yes, I think it must have been something like that. I stepped to the window. Looking down, I saw Amelia arm in arm with John Garvin, who was escorting her to a car. The hospital's insignia was prominent on the breast pocket of his coat. And probably for that reason as much as any, reveler Haligonians politely stepped aside and granted them leeway.

WE DON'T WANT TO LOSE HER

Journal entry January 7, 1919. 4:20 a.m. Halifax

"Adoption Papers"
"Tired Monk's Café"
"Joy and Sadness"

NINETEEN EIGHTEEN IS A WEEK DEPARTED, THOUGH joy and sorrow have no calendar, no boundaries in Time, as Heraclitus put it. The war is over; Spanish flu rages on. That very Armistice Day night last November when we'd returned to Halifax with the child, Amelia had gone back to work, as I have already described in this journal. Within a few weeks after that, I decided to stop writing for newspapers, a decision that included a lot of trepidation about how to make ends meet. But I had shifted my devotions to the child, and to my book about sleeplessness. Looking at what I've just now written, what a surprising sentence. But the main thing to say is, we kept the child. That may seem like promoting the obvious as a revelation, but it's nonetheless true. We heard nothing from Elsbeth Frame, or Josephine Huntley, or anybody else in Parrsboro. Clearly they were not going to contact us. There simply was no place for the child there. We had to look right at this.

"We keep not inquiring about an orphanage," I said one evening at dinner.

"Why do you think that is?"

"Because we don't want to be without her. Simple as that."

"But we'd long ago decided on not having a child."

"The child herself's changed our minds."

"When you look at her, does she remind you of anyone?"

"Do you mean do I associate her with Elizabeth Frame?"

"Her and everything else you saw at Petit-de-Grat. Because I don't have those associations, you see."

"I don't either. I'm completely present tense."

"Are you sure?"

"Yes. The child's put me entirely in the present tense."

"I'm in the present tense, too, but also in the future tense. I should have told you, Toby, but tomorrow they're delivering a new crib and a new bureau for her room. Also, I purchased two baby quilts. Plus some adorable clothes. Plus three knit caps."

"That'll make four knit caps. I bought one yesterday."

"I've told one person at hospital. I only said we have been living with a child. Andrea Sitwell, you haven't met her. I trust her. She swore herself to secrecy, so I didn't have to. She didn't need more information. You know, what do you mean 'living with'? Didn't even ask. Except she asked if I was happy. I said I was very happy."

"I've noticed."

"It feels like a moment to dance to. That's one of my own mother's original Scottish phrases. She didn't use it often."

"I've been meaning to ask. Where are the books we took from Oscar's apartment?"

"Oh, they're in a box on the shelf in the hallway closet. What made you suddenly think of that?"

"I don't know. I just thought of it."

I had modest savings; by that I mean I'd put frugality in the bank, as the saying goes. I had enough to pay monthly bills for at least a year, possibly eighteen months without my having other employment, unforeseen emergencies aside. I discovered the library; I did all manner of research; I filled notebooks. Amelia joked, "Lucky you, all you have to do is find people who can't sleep and write about that." And we kept the child. We pasted cutout stars and planets on the ceiling of her room. But we kept referring to her only as "the child." She was with us now. One evening, Amelia said, "The thing is, we're all she really has in the world, aren't we."

Then, on the night of December 30, Amelia came home at 8 p.m. from hospital in a frightful state. She sat at the kitchen table and didn't take off her coat. She waved off any conversation. She waved off a cup of coffee. She waved off holding the child. Finally, she said, "I'm sobbing without tears. I have to just sit here awhile. Leave me alone, please."

Later, I'd guess it was around 11 p.m., I sat across from her.

"Is the child asleep?" she said.

"Sound asleep, yes. You know, I think the sound of the typewriter's like a lullaby."

"Probably an actual lullaby is better. Do you know any?"

"I can learn some."

"Don't get me wrong. The typewriter may help her drift off. It's had that effect on me."

"What happened, Amelia? Just tell me."

"I lost a child in surgery today," she said, and completely broke down. She was broken. Her face was flushed, her eyes red, her face tear-streaked. "A year-old girl. I've seen everything. You know I have. But this was different."

"In what way different? I hardly know how to ask."

"Because of *our* child different. Because when I was in the midst of it, I knew the surgery was a last-ditch effort and there was every likelihood it would fail. Septicemia was running its course. And I saw it in the attendings' eyes—they'd hardly look at me. That terrible recognition, who can blame them. This little girl was about to end her full life. And then she was gone. Just like that, gone. She died and I had to walk to the waiting room and inform the parents. Then I went to my office. Did you know, the word *sepsis* was introduced in Homer's poems—I mean, that's for at least a couple thousand years. Also Hippocrates—he used it. I sat in my office, not fit for human company. And I thought, Why during surgery did I somehow feel this little girl had had a *full life*? Of course, it was a full life in the sense that it was as full as it would ever get. Of course that. But I also thought, We can't know what she actually experienced, right up to her last breath. What memories she might have even at that age, who knows. What her beating heart felt like to her. And then I realized mine was the last face she saw. You see, it's routine to lean in close and look at a patient's eyes before the anesthetic takes effect. How is that right? How is it right, that the last face she saw wasn't her mother's or father's, it's just not right."

We sat for a while not talking.

"I'm sorry. I get how difficult it was after that surgery to come home to the child in our house."

"Toby, can't you say *our* child? We have to say it. Because don't we feel that way? Equally, don't we feel that way? 'Ours.' Because if we don't equally, I will inquire at an orphanage."

"No need for that."

"Because *our* child—think how full her life has already been. Born as she was and to whom. Surrounded by Spanish flu in Petit-de-Grat. Imagine that! Then carried by strangers in an automobile across the province. We sat with her near driftwood on the beach, don't forget that. She heard seagulls. She's heard rain, and even hail, that one morning, don't forget that. She's even heard a war end outside on the street. These things happened. How can her life have been fuller thus far, if you really think about it, in a certain way."

"I get what you're saying. But I also think you need some sleep. Is there any chance of you sleeping?"

"I'm afraid I'll dream of what happened in surgery. I'd rather drink a hundred coffees than dream of that."

"How about a brandy?"

"That actually might work. But you have to lie down next to me."

Amelia slept until just after 9 a.m. Our child was in her bassinette in the kitchen.

Sipping coffee, Amelia said, "I dreamed of every single room in this house. I was like a museum docent or something. 'Here's the kitchen, here's the stairs to the attic.' At the kitchen table in the dream, I read a patient's file. But then guess what? I could tell it was the afternoon, I looked at a clock on the wall and it was three thirty. And in walked our child."

"What do you mean, *walked*?"

"She'd walked home from school. She walked into the house. She had a glass of water. She walked upstairs to her room."

"How old was she? In this dream of yours."

"I think about ten. Possibly eleven."

"Was I in this dream?"

"I heard the typewriter. I didn't get the impression I'd remarried. So it was probably you in the other room."

We looked at each other.

"We have to do something," she finally said. "Whatever it is, I can't stand it. I can't stand it another day. Not one more day. I'll go mad."

"Amelia, we need to legally adopt."

"How will we explain having our child with us already?"

"We say what happened. Maybe not everything, of course. But the basics of her getting orphaned. You're more than a solid upright citizen surgeon—more than reputable, apart from your choice of husband, maybe. You can obtain references from people from whom references make all the difference. I don't know all the legal whys and wherefores. But I have to think we'd be just fine."

"I know just the person to consult with. Frances Devereaux."

"The one that raised a million dollars for the war effort?"

"That's Frances. She's on the hospital board. Husband's a consultant to the prime minister. That sort of thing."

"We need to adopt our child—that sounds funny, but you know what I mean."

"How else to make an honest woman out of her?"

AFTER NEW YEAR'S DAY, government offices opened again on January 4, so first thing that morning we applied for adoption. As it turned out, bureaucratic paperwork took only a month. But still, I had to travel again up to Petit-de-Grat to get Dr. O'Shee to sign the official birth record. I had to borrow an automobile for this purpose. I was resigned to traveling there and back all in one trip; I had no intention of sleeping on a pew ever again, even if I had to drive half the night home.

In Petit-de-Grat, I simply knocked on the O'Shees' door, and when they both appeared on the porch, I just blurted out, "My wife and I are adopting the child born in your house." I had no earthly idea what their response might be.

"What about the grandmother?" Dr. O'Shee said.

"It wasn't meant to be. We're adopting."

"To each his own," Dr. O'Shee said.

I was not invited in but Mrs. O'Shee said, "That is lovely news. The child will be in a good home. What's her Christian name?"

"We haven't decided yet."

"Go back as far as you can—say to your wife's great-great-grandmother," Mrs. O'Shee said. "Go back far enough in a name, your child's less likely to be touched by Elizabeth Frame's nature. Not that the child would be, anyway. She's an innocent in all of this, isn't she."

Dr. O'Shee signed the document and shut the door without so much as another word. It didn't trouble me in the least. I had obtained what I'd come for, and little else mattered. Leaving Petit-de-Grat, I saw *Fiddler's Woe* anchored in harbor; Tennyson was on deck. I was happy to see he'd survived so far.

~

JUST AFTER NEW YEAR'S DAY, I'd had a stenography lesson from a woman named Denise Frost, who has worked as a court stenographer going on ten years. We met at Tired Monk's Café and sat at adjacent tables; she had her stenographic machine, a different model from the one I had purchased from Peter Lear. Denise is about thirty-five, I would guess.

"I really love my work," she said. "I feel like I'm doing something useful. Of course, a magistrate is my boss in court, but otherwise I feel quite independent in my work."

We each had a coffee and then she took me through the basics of the machine.

"I'll talk and you record now," she said after an hour or so. At which point she simply began describing what she saw in the café itself, chairs, tables, pastries and so forth, people, with a few humorous asides.

When she had finished she asked to see my transcript; she scrutinized it and said, "Your spelling is atrocious, but in getting down the words, you did all right, for a first time. My advice? Sit with your wife—you mentioned she's a surgeon—and let her talk about her day at the hospital, and you type away. It's all just practice practice practice."

I paid her the fee we had decided on and she left the café, and I stayed for a cheese Danish and another cup of coffee. I went home and sat with our child and Amelia went to the hospital.

That evening at dinner, I told Amelia about my lesson. She rubbed her hands together with delicious excitement and said, "Oh good, because you aren't going to believe what happened today at my work."

That evening's transcript scrolled out to twenty sections, each separated by a line of perforated dots.

"Let me see," Amelia said. She read five or six sections. "All these years we've been married," she said, "I never really noticed how bad your spelling is."

A week or so of practice on the machine followed, until I felt ready to put it to actual use. I had picked out my first subject for my book on sleeplessness, or insomnia, or whatnot. It was a woman named Esther Markham, age forty-four, who lived next door to Homer and Beatrice Orlen. I obtained her address from Homer along with a few paragraphs of information about Esther's son Zachary, who, during the last one hundred days of the war, was a casualty near the Canal de l'Escaut outside Cambrai. I posted a note to Esther at her address. I got a note back from her in merely eight days: *Dear Mr. Havenshaw, Come by at 4 p.m. any weekday. I am always home then.*

Before 1918, Esther had already been a widow for fifteen years. She alone had raised their son Zachary from age seven. When Zachary was eighteen, he became a sniper with the Fourth Canadian Mounted Rifles; once in France, he further trained with a Lebel rifle with APX Mle. 1917 scope, with a quick-release thumb latch. But he had also developed a specialty, and became known for his ability to pick off pilots in the gondolas of German barrage balloons—or kite balloons—which were primarily employed as aerial platforms for intelligence gathering or the spotting of artillery. These balloons were filled with hydrogen gas. Anyway, Zachary Markham not only could "shoot straight up in the air with deadly accuracy," but also could readily hit balloon pilots parachuting to earth. In August of 1918 Zachary was killed by a German sniper.

Homer has said, "Next door to us on Rosewood Street, Beatrice and I would look through the window and see Esther up at all hours. Beatrice and Esther are great friends. They confide. And at one point, a few months before Zachary was killed, Esther told Beatrice she no longer slept. Of course, a person has to sleep, but Esther only did at the odd hour and often while standing, she told Beatrice. She also told Beatrice that every night before her son died, she was 'kept awake by premonitions.'" I wrote that in my notebook: *Kept awake by premonitions.*

On a Thursday when Amelia had the day free to be with our child, at the appointed hour I walked over to meet with Esther Markham. I had the Universal Stenotype machine in tow. There were at least a dozen photographs of Zachary on the mantel over the fireplace. It would be too much a chore here to copy out that afternoon's transcript; I can say, however, it was evident that the conversation seemed to give her solace, but in turn clearly caused her great pain. We spoke for about an hour exclusively about her son. At one point she asked me if I'd served, and I told her why I hadn't. I half expected a judgment, but she said, "Had that only applied to Zack." Then I told her my intentions to write a book and told her its subject. "That's not a book I'd ever read," she said, "but I'm all right with contributing to it." And what I am compelled to write here in my journal is that hearing the torments and travails of Esther's insomnia really served to anchor my conviction that a book might be possible. What I heard from Esther about her "premonitions," her relentless visions of Zachary's demise, all sorts of things. "I don't know if Homer told you this," Esther had said, "but that day at nine o'clock in the morning, I told Beatrice that Zachary was gone. She protested but I was certain of it. And the telegram arrived to Homer at the *Standard* at 4 p.m. that same day. The War Office had Homer as the contact, you see. As the saying goes, 'A mother knows even before God knows.'"

⌒

THEN, ON FEBRUARY 5, we took our child to the appropriate government office and registered Emmeline Amelia Havenshaw. Emmeline, after Amelia's great-great-grandmother Emmeline.

The moment Amelia had suggested that name, there was no further discussion. We were in giddy agreement there.

The clerk said, "Information about the birth mother and father remains confidential."

"They're in separate cemeteries," Amelia said, which I could see slightly startled the clerk.

"That is to say," Amelia said, softening her tone, "we won't be hearing from them."

"I've been apprised of every sort of situation imaginable," the clerk said. "It's not uninteresting, often. But in the end, I'm just a clerk."

We walked some blocks and then ducked out of the cold into Tired Monk's Café on Morris Street. We each ordered hot cocoa. We stared at the piece of paper that declared our daughter's legal name. We sipped hot cocoa.

Looking around the café, Amelia said, "This will be our place. *Our* place. The three of us."

"Good," I said. "Home away from home." But Amelia drifted off. "Penny for your thoughts."

"I'll give them to you free of charge, darling." Amelia seemed to hold Emmeline ever closer. "It will sound strange, but it suddenly sunk in, what happened to us in 1918. What I saw and did in France. What you saw in Parrsboro and Petit-de-Grat. I can't consider it an unlikely story, ours. Because it all actually happened. So it's likely. But also, it just feels to me that what with the war, Spanish flu—what's Heraclitus say? Oh, yes, 'the soul's displacements'—really nothing happened to people in 1918 that was unlikely. And add to that, us three sitting here together."

Busy as a year in the Old Testament, I thought. But I didn't say it.

"Good Lord, what's made me so lofty?" Amelia said. "Insufferable. I have violins playing next to me all the time, don't I." She looked at her watch. "I've got to be at hospital in three quarters of an hour."

"I was thinking beef and vegetable stew for dinner."

"Perfect."

"No doubt an exhausting rest of the day ahead of you. Late dinner or not, doesn't matter. It'll be waiting."

"At first I might not be fit for human company. But something simple as a hot bath will turn that around."

"I have every confidence."

"Don't forget to pick up that lotion for Emmeline's dry skin. It's just her knees and elbows. Nothing whatsoever to worry about."

"J. H. Angwin's Apothecary's just two blocks."

"Maybe it's time—or soon—to have some friends over. You know, to present Emmeline. I've already posted a letter to family in Scotland. Let's have some photographs taken."

Sitting at the café table, the radiator making the occasional hollow clank but working effectively on a cold day, the front window partially steamed over, bread straight from the oven just set out on trays and the aroma wafting, Amelia blew on the surface of her hot cocoa, dipped her finger into the cup and tested it. "It's fine now," she said. With another touch of cocoa on the same finger, she let Emmeline have a taste. Wherever you sit, so sit all the insistences of fate. Still, the moment held promise of a full life.

ABOUT THE AUTHOR

Howard Norman received the Lannan Award in literature and was twice a finalist for the National Book Award in fiction. He is the author of ten novels, four memoirs, and award-winning books for children illustrated by Leo and Diane Dillon. He is writing a ten-episode graphic noir, *Detective Lev Detects*. His most recent memoir is *The Wound Is the Place the Light Enters You*, about the painter Jake Berthot. He lives in Vermont with his wife, poet Jane Shore.